GLIMMER

SUMMER'S HAREM BOOK 2

MAGGIE ALABASTER

Cover by Ravenborn designs

Edited by Lily Luchesi

For Lila, who is really Khat.

CHAPTER ONE

I stood up and rubbed my ass.

It must have borne the brunt when I'd been thrown out of the veil between the Fae world and this—the human world.

"Fletcher? Huon?" I turned in a slow circle. "Saff? Kale? Anyone?"

Five of us and Khat, the mimicat, had taken this journey together, in search of the second key. We already had the first, which should somehow unlock the door to release lesser magic back into the Fae realm and open the ordinary veil between the worlds. "Ordinary" because there was nothing normal about the vortex which spun me like a cork and separated me from my lovers and Khat.

I ducked behind a tree as a rumbling sound drew closer.

A car. I'd seen them plenty of times before when I came to this realm, but I never liked them. I wrinkled my nose. They smelled worse than the rotting foliage in the Fae realm.

The car sped past without slowing.

I held my breath for a while and wracked my mind for a moment.

Oh yes, suburbs. That was what humans called places like this. In some ways, it reminded me of the palace in the capital in the Fae realm. There, Fae lived close together, but still surrounded by nature. That was where the comparison ended, because we had no roads, or buildings made from bricks. We preferred wood, although our ancestors, the same ancestors we shared with the trolls, built in stone.

I kept to the path which led along the side of the road and walked slowly. My gaze shifted this way and that. The human realm was enormous, but surely my companions hadn't ended up too far from me?

"Please gods, let them be somewhere close," I muttered.

"Talking to yourself is frowned upon in the human world," a voice remarked.

I jumped. "Huon?" I looked around frantically, but saw no sign of the Fae king.

"Guess again." This time it was Saff's voice I heard.

I sagged slightly. "Khat."

"Don't sound so disappointed." This time the mimicat used my voice. He leapt down from the fence at the front of a large house. His tail swished back and forth.

I ignored his comment. "Have you seen the others?"

"Meow," he replied.

I arched an eyebrow at him.

"Talking cats are also frowned upon." He sounded annoyed. His ears twitched.

"As long as no one hears you…" I glanced around. "So, have you?"

"No," he replied. "This is not where the veil usually leads to. I have no idea where we are."

He sounded so defeated, my heart melted toward him a little. All he wanted was to be reunited with his mimicat mate and their kittens, who were stuck here.

My sympathy diminished somewhat when he said, "Maybe the guys are dead. That would be extremely inconvenient."

"That's one way to put it," I said dryly. "We might be stuck here forever."

"In theory, yes." He stretched out on the grass in a patch of sun. "I'll have to spend the rest of my life pretending I'm a normal cat." He sounded disgusted, but he looked comfortable enough.

I sighed. "And I would have to shrink down and look like a tiny insect. At least you don't have wings to hide."

"You could grow huge and pretend you're a god," Khat said helpfully.

I grimaced. "I don't think things are quite so desperate."

"Yet."

"Yet," I agreed. "All right, we need to find the guys. I don't suppose you have some sort of tracking magic?"

He rolled onto his back and rubbed himself against the grass. "If I did, would I be here talking to you?"

"Probably not. Why are you?" He was starting to get on my nerves now.

He rolled back over and sat up. "Because we need each other, like it or not. I have no desire to be stuck here forever, pretending to be a housecat."

"Now we've cleared that up, how are we going to

find the others?" I ran a hand over my head and tugged at the end of my hair.

"Tavar could probably have found them." She was back in the Fae realm, guarding the veil we came through.

"She would have stood out faster than you if you spread your wings," he pointed out. "Although I have seen humans dress up to look like monsters and things, so maybe she'd fit right in."

"She's a troll, not a monster," I said dryly.

"Her kind eats my kind," he replied darkly. "I stand by what I said."

"It's moot anyway, since she's not here." I released my hair and dropped my hand. "Humans have ways of finding each other. Maybe we could look up Fletcher's address and he could come and get us."

"Assuming he found his way back to his house. That could be on the other side of the world from here."

I groaned. "What do you suggest then?"

"Shit!" Khat rose and streaked up into a tree.

"What the hells?" I whirled around to see a very large dog. With what I hoped was a firm hold on the animal's leash, was a man with tattoos from his wrists to the sleeves of his black t-shirt. His angular chin was covered in a layer of stubble. His brown hair was tied back from his face.

I caught all of that in a glance, but most of my attention was on the dog.

I backed up a few steps, my hands raised. I had rarely seen dogs up close and never this big. I froze when the dog stopped to sniff at me.

"It's all right, Tiny doesn't bite." The man tugged on his leash, but the dog ignored him.

For a moment I didn't comprehend what he was saying. When I did, I blinked.

"Its name is Tiny?" I raised the tip of my finger and pointed toward the enormous dog.

"Him," the man corrected with a smile. "Yes. It's an ironic name."

"That it is," I muttered. I eyed the dog as he looked up toward the tree Khat fled to.

"He's harmless, really. Do you want to pat him?" The man gave me a lop-sided smile.

I stared at the man. He was a good looking guy. I was concerned the dog might try to eat me, and not in the way I like to be eaten, but I took a moment to appreciate the view.

"Pat him?" I echoed.

"Yeah." He ran a hand across Tiny's head, which

was two or three times larger than his hand. "He likes it, see?"

Tiny seemed more interested in Khat than being patted, but I shook my head anyway.

"I'm sure he's nice and all that, but I think I'll pass, thank you." I gave him a nervous smile and laugh. "Can you tell me where we are? I'm so lost."

He considered for a moment before he nodded. "It happens to the best of us. Even Tiny from time to time. He always comes back though. He's a smart bugger, even if he looks like a dumbass." He patted the dog again.

"So—about where we are?" I realised then he spoke in the same accent as Fletcher. That gave me some hope.

"Bell's Hill," The man replied. "Y'know, in Sydney. Although, my dad used to say we're so far out, it might as well be whoop-whoop. Still, it's all right out here, when the trains run and all that."

Sydney? If I recalled my human realm geography, that was in Australia. On the west, no, east coast. Fletcher was from Australia. That was promising. How big could one country be, after all?

"I don't suppose you know a man named Fletcher Remington. He's a friend of mine. I'm looking for him."

"Is he your boyfriend?" the man asked, a teasing smile on his lips.

"You could say that," I said, flushing slightly. "So, do you know him?"

"Nope. I can Google him if you like?"

"Google?" I echoed. "Is that magic of some kind?"

His eyes widened and he laughed. "You're funny. This Fletcher guy is a lucky man."

"Um, thanks."

Without explaining what a google was, he pulled something out of his pocket. I'd seen phones before and recognised this as one.

"All right, let's see..." He held the leash in one hand, the phone in the other and tapped at the screen with his thumb.

Tiny eyed me dubiously. I gave him the same in return. He might have stayed put, but Khat chose that moment to sneeze.

The dog let out a tremendous bark and lunged toward the tree. The leash slid out of the man's grip. Tiny leapt at the tree, barking and growling.

"Oh shit!" The man ran toward him and tried to pick up the end of the leash. The dog kept leaping, which pulled the leash out of his reach every time he almost grabbed it. "Hold still, you dumbass!"

Khat sat perched on a branch, just out of reach.

He arched his back and hissed at the dog, which only made the bark more.

Apparently tired of the attention, Khat sat back and said, "Oh go away, you stupid animal."

The man's mouth dropped open. He gestured toward Khat. "What the fuck? That cat talked!"

He finally managed to grab Tiny's leash and pull him back from the tree. "Say something else," he insisted.

Khat blinked. "Meow."

He looked over her shoulder at me. "You heard it, right?"

I licked my lips. I couldn't tell him the truth, but I didn't want him to think he was going crazy either.

"I…"

The man shook his head. "I've been clean for years. Not even an aspirin. I'm not trippin'. That cat talked." His eyes begged me to confirm he'd heard what he had.

"So what if I did?" Khat asked.

The man whirled back around. "See? You heard it that time, right?"

"I'm a he, and of course she heard me. She has perfectly good hearing." Khat's tail flicked. "My name is Khat, who are you?"

I sighed. For a moment there, I thought we might

get some help from this man. If Khat had just kept his mouth shut...

"I'm Jude. How can you talk?"

"I open my mouth and words come out," Khat said facetiously. "Also I can do this," he added, mimicking my voice.

Jude turned back to me. "Are you a ventriloquist?"

"I beg your pardon?" I asked, taken aback.

"You're talking, but it looks like the cat is talking," Jude replied. "Is he a puppet?"

Khat and I spoke at the same time.

"Yes."

"Most certainly not."

I rubbed my forehead. "Look, we really don't have time for this. I need to find my friends—"

"Boyfriends," Khat interjected.

"Yes, well... We need to find them."

"You and your puppet?" Jude asked doubtfully.

"I am *not* a puppet." Khat now spoke in Jude's voice. "Perhaps now you will understand. I am real and we require assistance."

A lesser Fae or human might have run away from this crazy situation. The gods knew I would have if I could.

To his credit, Jude stood his ground. He eyed Khat for a long while. "He's real?" he asked finally.

"Yes," I replied. "He's a very real cat, who just happens to talk. It's…normal where I'm from."

"Perfectly normal," Khat agreed. "And normally perfect, if I say so myself."

I arched an eyebrow at him, but didn't contradict him. "I can explain, but it will take some time."

Jude licked his lips. "I might regret this, but maybe we could talk about it over a coffee? There's a cafe at the end of the street. They don't mind Tiny, so they might not be bothered by a weird, talking cat."

"I'm a perfectly un-weird mimicat."

"Un-weird? Is that even a word?" I asked.

"It is now," Khat replied, his nose in the air.

"Is mimicat a word?" Jude asked.

I sighed again. "I think we have a lot to talk about." Thank the gods, I would get coffee.

CHAPTER TWO

"Can I get the strongest coffee you have, in the biggest cup you have?" I asked.

"I'm pretty sure that's a soup mug," Jude said as we carried our steaming beverages over to an outside table.

Tiny was curled up beside it, eyes closed. His tongue lolled out as he panted.

"I don't care," I replied. I had to hold the mug in both hands and push the chair back from the table with my foot. "I haven't had coffee in the longest time." The smell made my mouth water.

"They don't have coffee in talking-cat land?" Jude slid into the chair beside me and smiled over his cup.

"As a matter of fact, they don't," I said sadly. "It

won't grow... Wait a minute, what makes you think there's a talking-cat land?"

"The talking cat is the first clue," he replied. "If a cat could talk, it would usually be an internet sensation."

I gave him a blank look.

He waved it off with one hand. "It doesn't matter, but keep an eye on him. He'd be worth millions if anyone catches him and films him talking."

"Not a chance," Khat said from under the table. He must have curled up beside Tiny, who evidently no longer cared about trying to chase him. "I've been here before. I know how to avoid being caught."

A server walked by and started clearing the table beside ours.

"Meow," Khat said.

"Smooth," I muttered ironically.

"I thought so. I mean, meow."

I glanced over to the server, but she gave no sign of having heard. I sipped my coffee and waited for her to leave.

"Second, you have no idea what Google is," Jude said. "Or you're good at faking it."

"I never fake it," I replied.

His eyebrows quirked. "I'm sure you don't."

I half expected Fletcher or Saff to appear and

give my comment an innuendo rating, as I had done to them, but neither did.

"Lastly," Jude went on after a few moments, "I've never heard an accent like yours."

"I could just be from far away," I argued. "Like, really far away."

He pressed his cups to his lips and watched me while he drank.

"It's the cat, isn't it?" I asked. "It's not any of the rest of it, just the cat."

"It's a little bit the rest of it," he assured me, "but it's ninety-nine percent the cat."

"If he'd just kept his mouth shut." I put down my mug and sighed. "What are you going to do?" I doubted the human realm authorities would look kindly on one of my kind. Assuming they could catch me, that was. I wouldn't allow that, no matter what it took.

"What was that name you wanted me to search up? Fletcher something?"

I was taken aback. "You're still going to help me?"

"That depends, are you here to overthrow our governments and take over the world?" he asked.

"No," I replied quickly. "I'm not here to hurt anyone."

"Shame," he replied in a tone which made me

wonder if he hadn't been at least a bit hopeful. "Not about hurting people. I just thought a talking cat might make a better..." He shook his head. "Never mind."

"I *would* make a better leader," Khat said. "You should all bow down to me."

"Not going to happen," I told him.

He huffed and fell silent.

"Anyway." I drew the word out. "I just need to find the others—"

"How many others?" Jude looked nervous now.

"An invasion fleet," Khat said.

I rolled my eyes. "Four. Well, three; Fletcher is from the human realm."

"Any more talking cats?"

"Yes, I'm raising an army of them to—"

I cut Khat off. "His mate and some kittens got stuck here." If he was going to help, I might as well tell him what we were facing. I explained about the taint on the Fae realm, how dark magic sucked lesser magic into a locked vault and how we needed the keys to release it. I left out the part about the trolls and Tavar. He had enough to absorb without me bringing them into it.

"We found the first key and a smaller version of the veil which brought us here, but we got separated somehow." I picked up my mug and sipped. The coffee was getting cold, but it still tasted amazing.

"Without this—Kale, and the first key, you can't find the second?" Jude asked.

I had to give him credit. He didn't look as though he thought I was going crazy.

"The key seems to know where the others are." I nodded. "At least, in his hands. He's the foretold, or so the ancient souls in the vault said."

For some reason, that still bothered me. Huon and I were given the task to return lesser magic to the Fae realm by Huon's father, Birch, on his deathbed. One of us should be chosen, if anyone was.

I knew it was childish and irrational to think that way. I had my own role to play in this task, we all did. This whole thing was much more important than my silly ego.

"You have no way to find the other—what did you call them—Fae?" Jude asked.

I pressed my fingertips to my temple and shook my head. "None. If we all found Fletcher, we could find each other though."

"Right," Jude said slowly. He pulled his phone back out and pressed on the screen.

"Fletcher Remington," I reminded him.

"Okay, I'll start in Sydney. Let's see here... A.A. Remington, Beth Remington, C.S and D.T Remington, R.L. Remington... No Fletcher. Not even an F. Remington."

My heart sank. Then it rose and began to hammer. "He has a brother named Rick. They share a house."

"R.L. could be Rick," Jude agreed. "It could also be Rachel, but we won't know until we go there."

"We?" Khat asked.

"If you need a toilet, don't do it under the table," Jude said.

I chuckled.

Khat seemed less amused. "This is why the human realm needs to be overthrown."

I peered under the table. "Is that why you came here?"

"No, but now I'm here—hey!"

Tiny, having seen me looking, wagged his huge tail and hit Khat in the face.

Khat hissed, but Tiny went on wagging.

I sat back up. "I appreciate the coffee and the help, but if you can just tell me how to find this Rick, I can find my way there?"

"You have a car?" Jude asked. "Or money for a train?"

"No, but—"

"How will you get there then? Fly?" He looked amused.

"As a matter of fact…"

His face paled. "If someone sees you, they'll…"

"I can fly without being seen," I told him.

"You can go invisible?" He looked impressed.

"No, but I can change my size." I told him how I escaped from the place I'd found Fletcher by shrinking small enough to fit through a crack. "I'll be the size of a bug."

"That's a handy trick, but I'd feel better if I could take you there myself." He hesitated. "It's been a while since I've felt useful. I got laid off from my last job and I haven't found another."

"We're trying to save our world, not provide support services to wayward humans," Khat said scathingly.

Jude's face dropped.

After an uncomfortable silence, I said, "All right, you can come. I don't want to get lost again anyway."

He perked up. "Great. My car should fit us all. You might have to put Khat on your lap though. The back seat is Tiny's."

I ignored Khat's grumbling from under the table

and smiled. "Deal, but he better keep his claws to himself."

"I make no promises," Khat said darkly.

"We *could* leave him behind," I suggested.

"Don't you dare," Khat replied. He stepped out from under the table. "You need me."

"What for, commentary on my life?"

"Wisdom," he replied, just as he plopped back down and started to lick his genitals.

I snorted. "That's one word for it. Still, it would be better to stay together until we find the others." Khat would probably disappear the moment he found his mate, but until then, he was the only one who understood what was at stake. Under that sarcastic exterior, he wanted to save the Fae realm as much as I did.

"Are you going to finish your coffee?" Jude asked.

It was cold now, but I gulped the rest down like a woman starving for air. If I had to be stuck here, at least I could drink this stuff. Whatever forces cut the Fae realm off from this were cruel indeed.

I placed the cup back on the table with regret. If I could, I would have another, but we had no time for that. We had to find R.L Remington and hope to the gods he was related to Fletcher, or at least knew where to find him.

CHAPTER THREE

"*I* thought it was close by," I said.

We'd returned to Jude's house and piled into his car. Tiny had stretched out on the back seat and started to drool. Khat had curled up on my lap and looked to have fallen asleep. Every now and again, his paw or tail would twitch.

I guessed he was dreaming about his mate and their kittens, but he could be thinking about his plans for world domination for all I knew.

While he drove, Jude explained the internet and what it meant to go viral. Those might be all Khat could hope for. If I had my way, he wouldn't even get that. Most humans didn't know about the Fae realm and we wanted to keep it that way.

"It is close," Jude replied. "By city standards."

I looked toward the map on the dashboard of his car. A blue dot marked R.L.'s address and a red line showed our route there. If I had to guess, I'd say it was a five minute flight. We'd been sitting in the car, stopping and starting, for at least two hours.

"If we'd get a few bloody green lights," Jude growled and the car stopped again.

"Is it unusual for them to be red every time?" I asked. I knew from past visits that green meant go and orange meant different things to different drivers. Some stopped, others went faster.

"Not really," he replied. "I think they make 'em red so much to make people take trains."

"Would that be faster?" I asked.

"Depends if the trains are running or not," he replied.

"Oh, I see," I said, although I didn't. As far as I could tell, cities were smelly and full of people living wingtip to wingtip. Or elbow to elbow. Whatever.

"It shouldn't be much longer." Jude rolled his shoulders, then sat forward again. "Come on dick-head, the light is green!"

The car moved forward with a jerk and we passed through the intersection. The buildings on either side were low, but most looked old and worn out. Some were closed, with boards over the front.

One sold cars, which were somehow *inside* the building. Maybe they had magic here after all.

We passed before I could ask about it, and turned into a street full of small houses.

"Now we just need somewhere to park." Jude sounded frustrated. "That's the problem with these old streets. There's never anywhere to put a car."

"What about in your pocket?" I asked.

He glanced at me quickly, then back at the road. "That would be handy," he said with a laugh.

"I mean, I could do it if you like," I said. "It shouldn't come to any harm if I shrink it."

The car jerked to a stop.

He twisted around and stared. "Can you unshrink it afterward?"

"Of course."

He tapped the steering wheel with one hand. "We should go somewhere no one can see you do it."

"I can't see anyone around," I pointed out.

"Unless someone is watching from inside a house." He kept tapping and looked uncertain.

"What would happen if they do?" Khat asked. "No one would believe them if they told anyone."

"They might film it," Jude said. "Although, they'd probably put it down to some new technology of some kind."

"There we go then." I undid my seatbelt and opened the door. Khat leapt off my lap before I climbed out after him. Jude unharnessed Tiny and attached his leash.

The moment he closed the door behind the huge dog, I gave a flick of my fingers and the car shrank to the size of a child's toy.

Awe on his face, Jude crouched and stared at the car. "Bloody hell, that's amazing."

Tiny sniffed at the car and looked ready to eat it before Jude snatched it up.

"I don't want to have to dig my car out of your shit," he told the dog. He tucked it away in a pocket. "I hope it won't leak oil on me."

"Oops," Khat slunk off to a patch of overrun grass to pee. "Didn't think of that, did you?"

"I don't know anything about cars," I admitted.

Jude patted his pocket. "I'm sure it will be fine. I hope so, I don't think my insurance covers 'act of fairy'."

"Fae," I corrected.

"What's the difference?"

"Fairies are fictional," I replied.

"Until today, I would have said Fae were too." He glanced over to me as we stepped off the road.

"Some Fae think humans aren't real," I remarked.

"They're something used to scare children into behaving."

"That's trolls," Khat said.

"It's both, but trolls are real." I ducked under a gnarled tree branch. Even as dried as it looked, it was still healthier than many of those back home.

"I'm pretty sure humans are real too," Jude said.

"That's true," Khat remarked. "No one could make you up."

"He's charming, isn't he?" Jude said sarcastically.

"That's one word for him," I agreed.

"I am the soul of charm," Khat said, looking piqued.

"You are soul all right," I replied.

Jude chuckled. "Arsehole. Good one."

I flashed him a smile. "Now, what number were we looking for?"

"Number four," Jude replied.

"There's one and three." I pointed. "Why is five next?"

"Humans only use odd numbers, because they're odd," Khat said.

"Odd numbers on one side of the road. Even on the other." Jude waved across the street. "There's four there."

"I have to agree with Khat on this one," I said. "That is strange."

"I third that," Jude agreed. "It must have made sense to someone." He started across the street. I followed close behind.

Number four was made of dark brown brick and thick, wooden window frames. Bushes obscured much of the lower floor, but as we drew closer, I saw each pane was topped with sections of coloured glass, as was the front door.

The door was covered by a screen door, which didn't open when I turned the handle.

"We need to ring the bell," Jude explained.

While I looked around for one, he pressed a button attached to the wall.

Ding dong.

I jumped. "What in the name of the gods?"

Jude chuckled. "That's the doorbell."

"That doesn't look like a bell." I eyed it doubtfully.

"At least it doesn't play *La Cucaracha*."

I was about to ask what he was talking about when the door swung inward.

"What?" The man bore a striking resemblance to Fletcher, but his face was clean shaven. They shared the same eye colour, but where Fletcher's were soft and kind, these were hard and cold. His hair was cut close to his head, but that looked to be the same shade as well.

He looked me up and down. If he'd noticed Jude or Tiny, he gave no sign. Where Khat had gone, I wasn't sure.

"If you're selling religion, fuck off," he snarled. "I don't need that shit here."

"I'm not selling anything," I said quickly. "I'm looking for a friend."

He regarded me, his expression unreadable. "I don't need any more friends. Unless you put out. In which case, come in and take your clothes off."

I rolled my eyes. If I didn't need to speak to him, I might have blown him up with my magic. I wouldn't rule out doing that later though.

"I'm looking for Fletcher. Do you know where he is?"

The man, I presumed he was Rick, scowled. "I have no idea where the fucker is. Haven't seen him for a few days. Why? Did he knock you up and take off?" His eyes wandered down to my stomach.

"No, he—" I sighed. I couldn't very well explain the situation to this man. I doubted he'd believe it anyway. "It doesn't matter. I guess I'll keep looking." I stepped back from the door.

"Have you tried calling him?" Jude asked.

"Do I look like a dickhead?" Rick asked. "Of course I have."

"Recently?" Jude pressed. "In the last hour or two?"

"What the fuck difference would that make? It keeps saying he's out of range."

"Maybe he's in range now." I wasn't exactly sure what they were talking about, but it seemed the right thing to say.

Rick gave a grunt and pulled a phone out of his pocket.

Does every human carry one of these things?

He pressed the screen and held it to his ear. His expression soon turned to surprise.

"Fletcher, you motherfucker. Where have you been? Where are you? There's some cute piece come looking for you. Blonde, about five-foot-five, legs for days. Tits the size of—yeah, that sounds like her."

My heart leapt. "Where is he?"

Rick looked up at me. "On the train. Reckons he'll be home soon. You better come in. Not the dog." That was the first indication he'd noticed Jude's presence.

"I'll tie him up out here." Jude looked furious. I suspected it was because Fletcher's brother was being a dick to me, rather than because he had to

27

leave his dog outside. Maybe it was because of both. Rick certainly wasn't like his brother in personality.

Fletcher mentioned he and his brother didn't get long. Now I knew why.

Rick unlocked the screen door and pushed it open before he disappeared inside. I assumed he expected me to follow, so I did.

Inside, the house was large and full of more light than I'd have expected from the outside. The furniture was all solid and looked well-used but sturdy. Some of it appeared as old as my one hundred and twenty three years. From what I knew of humans, that made it valuable.

"Coffee?" Rick asked.

"Uh, yes please." I tried not to sound too excited at the prospect of another cup.

"What's your name?" He walked to the kitchen at the back of the house and flicked on an electric kettle.

"Summer," I replied. I stopped to look at photographs on the walls. Several were of a younger Fletcher and his brother. Some showed a man and a woman I presumed were their parents.

"Well, you're hot enough. I'm Rick. You sure you won't reconsider that fuck? We have time before

Fletcher gets back. Just leave your boyfriend outside."

"He's not my boyfriend," I replied.

"Even better." Rick gave me a grin which might have been attractive if he wasn't being so slimy.

"Do you talk like that to all the girls?" I asked.

"Only the cute ones," he replied.

"Does it ever work?"

His expression fell. "Nope. I keep trying."

"Just a suggestion then," I said, as nicely as I could, "stop trying so hard."

He shrugged and spooned coffee into three cups. "It's who I am. Love me or leave me."

That was an easy choice. I couldn't imagine loving anyone so aggressive. I could imagine him touching me though. He looked like a man who knew how to—

I gave myself a mental head shake.

Jude came in and stood beside me. We shared glances and grimaces. If Rick wasn't Fletcher's brother, I would have left already. Huon could be a dick at times, but not like this.

"Sugar?" Rick asked.

"No thanks, I like it dark and bitter," I replied.

"Like my heart." Rick handed me a cup. "We might get along after all."

I smirked and inhaled the smell. If we were able to return home, I was going to take a bag of beans back with me. A *big* bag. Maybe two. Or several.

"I'm sure you're not that bad," I told him.

"I'm all that and worse, babe." Rick raised his mug to me and sipped.

"You're not much like your brother, are you?" I asked.

His eyes hardened further. "Why would I be? He was the golden child of the family. The perfect one. Never put a foot out of line. How fucking dull is that?"

"There's nothing wrong with doing the right thing," Jude interjected.

Rick snorted. "You don't exactly look like the poster boy for behaving like an angel."

"No, I wasn't," Jude agreed. "But I changed."

"Well good for you." Rick rolled his eyes. "You're not one of those do-gooders, are you?" He used air quotes with his spare hand. "*I turned my life around, you can too.*"

"Nope," Jude replied. "Live however you want. I'm just here to help my friend."

Rick opened his mouth to retort, but the door swung open and closed.

A moment later I was caught up in Fletcher's

firm and warm embrace, his mouth on mine. His tongue swept across my lips. They parted to let him inside and my tongue greeted his.

I wanted to melt there and then, but I reluctantly pulled back.

"Here you are. Have you found the others?" I searched his eyes.

Fletcher had had a hopeful expression until I asked that. Then it faded. "I thought they were with you."

I shook my head slowly. "I found Khat. He's outside somewhere. I have no idea where the others are."

Fletcher sagged and rubbed his chin.

"You look like shit," Rick remarked. "When did you grow that beard? What the hell is going on?"

Fletcher kept an arm around me and turned to face his brother. "It's nice to see you too," he said sarcastically. "I need to have a shower and change, then I'll explain everything."

"Everything?" I glanced over at him. He gave me a nod.

"Yes. We can trust Rick."

I raised an eyebrow at him. "Excuse me if I'm not so sure."

"Are you all into drugs?" Rick asked. He held his

hands up to either side of his face. "Because I don't want to be involved in that crap."

Fletcher put a hand on his shoulder. "It's nothing like that. I promise." He gave Jude a questioning look.

"We can trust Jude," I said firmly.

"If you trust him, then I do too," Fletcher replied. His eyes silently begged me to offer the same to him and his brother.

I couldn't do that, not right away, but I nodded. I would try, it was clearly important to him. He, in turn, was important to me.

I waved him away with a smile. "Go and wash. We have a lot to talk about."

"That we do," Fletcher agreed. "I think we'll need something stronger than coffee."

I held my cup to my chest. "After I've finished this." Nothing would part me from it, not even wine.

"I would never get between a woman and her coffee," Fletcher assured me.

"Wise man," Jude muttered. They shared a grin, while Rick scowled.

I sipped but sighed inwardly. Rick might look like Fletcher, but that was where the resemblance ended. One was sweet and the other sour. If only they weren't both so gods damned hot.

CHAPTER FOUR

"That's it. Now I know you're stoned."
Rick scowled at us.

"I don't know anything about the Fae realm, but I've seen her talking cat, and her magic." Jude pulled his car out of his pocket and held it in his palm. "See?"

Rick gave him a sarcastic smile. "It's a toy."

"I can make that go back to full size," I said dryly.

"Please, not in the middle of my house." Fletcher's hand hadn't moved from my knee since we sat down.

"How about I shrink your brother instead?" I smiled sweetly.

"Now that I can get behind," Fletcher nodded.

"I third that," Jude said.

"How about you don't?" Rick snarled. He hesitated for a moment. "If you really can do magic, shrink your wine glass."

"And don't blow it up," Fletcher teased.

I grinned. "I'll try not to. At least it's only wine and not coffee."

"True. Save your blowing for other things." Fletcher winked.

I considered for a moment. "Six. You've done better."

"That's true." He grinned. "I've *done* a lot better." He winked at me and my heart flipped. "The best, I'd say."

"Now that's an eight." I covered my hand with his and squeezed. "You get bonus points for flattery."

"And yet, the score of ten remains elusive." He sighed exaggeratedly.

"Of course, it can't be too easy." I reached for my wine glass. With a flourish, I made the glass and its contents shrink down to the size of my thumb tip. I tried not to look too smug as I passed it to Rick.

He took the glass and held it up to his eyes. "What the absolute crazy, fucked up shit is this?" He looked at me as though I might have a full-sized wine glass, complete with Cabernet Sauvignon, up my sleeve.

"Magic," I replied. "It's a pretty simple—"

"Undo it." He put the glass back on the table and pushed it back to me.

I touched it with a fingertip and it grew back to normal size. For good measure, I picked it up and took a sip. "It's nice wine."

"It really is," Fletcher agreed.

Rick slumped down in his chair. He looked pale.

I almost felt sorry for him. Almost.

"You're not shitting me?" He blinked rapidly a few times.

"Nope. This is totally legit." Fletcher smelled like soap and clean fabric. He trimmed his beard so it was neat and even. It covered his scars, white hairs peppered here and there.

As much as I liked his scruffy appearance, I preferred him like this. He looked comfortable and his short sleeves showed his muscular arms better than his hoody had.

"There's a world full of fairies?" Rick asked.

"Fae," I replied firmly. "And trolls."

"Not like on the internet," Fletcher said. "These trolls can be reasoned with."

"And fairies have wings?" Rick didn't seem to have heard what either Fletcher or I had said.

"Fae," I repeated. "Fae have wings. Trolls don't."

"They do walk around with no shirts on," Fletcher remarked.

Rick frowned at him, then looked back at me. "Can I see your wings?"

"Sure." I slipped off the jacket I wore to hide them. The shirt underneath had sections left open so they could fit through. Although they were a sensitive part of me, the Fae realm was rarely cold enough to need them covered to keep them warm.

Both Jude and Rick gasped as I stretched the multicoloured skin to its full span.

Jude looked awed, but Rick shook his head and put a hand over his eyes. He rubbed at his forehead with his fingertips and exhaled loudly.

"Why can't you have normal girlfriends?" he asked Fletcher.

Fletcher grinned. "Why have normal when you can have Fae?"

"I'm normal for a Fae," I said, while trying not to take offence at the question. I tucked my wings away and threw my jacket back over them.

"I've seen enough of the Fae world to know you're anything but ordinary," Fletcher assured me. He gave me a soft look that made my heart melt a little more.

Rick made a gagging sound.

I ignored him. "We need to find the others."

"If they ended up in the same place, then Kale would have found someone to help them get here, like you did," Fletcher reasoned.

"And if they didn't, they could be lost, the gods only know where." I took another sip of wine to calm my nerves.

"Gods are real?" Rick asked, as though he preferred not to know the answer.

"That's debatable," I replied. "But it's a conversation for another time." I turned back to Fletcher. "If Kale makes it here, we can find the key. Huon and Saff should feel the veil reopen and know to come home."

That left too many 'what ifs,' and I preferred to have everyone together in one place. We'd needed everyone to find the last key, and the small veil to the human realm. It may be we needed us all for this too.

Not to mention I'd feel better if I knew they were safe.

"It's getting late," Jude remarked. "I should get going."

"There's plenty of room." Fletcher ignored Rick's scowl. "You can put your dog in the laundry. It's big enough. And he might warn us if Kale or the others come."

"You know how Mum and Dad felt about animals inside the house," Rick said.

Fletcher flinched. "They're not here anymore. If he's left out there, someone will knock him off."

I gave him a questioning look.

"They'll steal him," he explained.

"Oh. Well, we don't want that." I nodded.

"If you're sure." Jude looked uncertain.

"Absolutely. There's a spare room upstairs. Summer can share with me. If she wants to?" Fletcher looked at me hopefully.

"Of course she does." I gave him a long look which I hope he understood. The last time we fucked, we were in a hurry, overwhelmed by lust. I wanted to take some time to explore each other.

Every. Single. Centimetre.

He smiled.

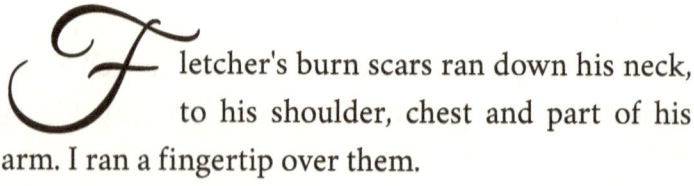

letcher's burn scars ran down his neck, to his shoulder, chest and part of his arm. I ran a fingertip over them.

"Was it your brother who pushed you into the fire?" I asked gently.

He gave a soft snort. "I can see how you'd come to that conclusion, but no, it wasn't him."

"A friend of his?"

"Something like that." He sighed. "It was a long time ago. I don't remember much about it. I mean, I've done my best to forget it. I get flashes from time to time, but those are more than enough." He shook his head slightly as if that might dislodge the memories forever.

"Would you mind if I said your scars were hot?" I sat on his bed, my bare feet tucked up beside me.

"I don't mind," he replied. "It's nicer than if you said they were ugly."

"Is that what you think?" I kept running my finger over them.

He shrugged his opposite shoulder. "Yeah, I guess so. I've spent most of my life hiding them. I won't even swim without a shirt on. Then again, I usually surf and that needs a wetsuit of some kind anyway, so they're covered, except my face."

"Wetsuit?" I quirked an eyebrow.

"Yeah, it's a rubber suit to keep you warm in the water."

"Ah. Yes it's much better to be warm and wet than

cold and wet," I said.

He smiled. "I give that a nine. For accuracy."

"Only a nine?" I pouted.

"It would be a ten, but we're only talking about it." He wrapped an arm around me, drew me close and pressed his mouth to mine.

I lay back and pulled him down with me. He covered my body with his. I wrapped my legs around him. He ground himself against me, drawing a moan from between my lips.

"I think our clothes are in the way," I said. He had discarded his shirt, but he still wore jeans.

I lowered my legs to the bed and slipped my hands between us to undo his button and slide down the zipper. I shoved them down as far as I could reach, and his bright blue boxers with them.

He kicked them aside.

"That takes care of me," he said, his voice husky. "It must be your turn." He slipped his hand under the hem of my top and over my stomach, rucking the fabric up as he went. He lightly massaged the skin under my breasts and around them, leaving them until last.

He shoved my top up to expose them, and my pebbled nipples.

"So beautiful," he breathed.

"You think?" I asked. "I think you are."

I sat up just enough to slip my top off and throw it aside.

He lifted himself up onto his elbow and looked at me, his brow slightly creased.

"Gods, you're gorgeous. Are you sure you want to be seen with a guy like me?"

"I'm very sure." I took his hand and pressed it to my breast. "Now shut up and kiss me."

He chuckled. "Yes ma'am." His fingers lightly caressed my breast as he lowered himself down to kiss me again. His lips were firm and hungry, and tasted like mint. His beard tickled. How would it feel against the tender flesh between my thighs?

He rolled my nipple between his thumb and fore-finger, sending a jolt of heat right to my core. Something about him made me drenched so fast.

Talk about getting warm and wet.

I curled my hand around his cock. It was hot in my fingers, hard and big, with a slight curve to the left.

I slid my hand up and down slowly, from his tip to his balls and back. I ran my thumb over his tip, slippery with pre-cum.

"If you keep doing that, I won't last long," he grunted.

His mouth left mine. He kissed his way down my neck, collarbone, chest, until he closed his mouth over one of my nipples. He flicked his tongue against it and began to suck gently.

At the same time, he ran a hand down my leg and between my thighs, squeezing the tender flesh and pushing my legs apart. He bent one of my knees and pressed it down to the mattress to open me up to him.

"Beautiful." He slid a finger inside me, then another.

"You're not wrong about being wet," he whispered.

"That's how much I want you." I pumped him a little harder with my hand.

"Fuck, woman." He thrust once, twice, then grabbed my wrist. "I won't make it that far if you keep doing that."

"Well then.…." I removed my hand and pushed him onto his back. I straddled his hips and lowered my pussy onto the tip of his cock. "We don't want to waste a moment."

He murmured something incoherent.

I took that as a good sign and lowered myself all the way down to his balls. The way he filled me made me want to scream.

He looked up at me and cupped my breasts in his hands. "You're so beautiful," he breathed. He rubbed my nipples with his palms.

"You're pretty hot yourself," I replied. I rose and came back down, slowly at first. Gradually increasing speed.

I ran a hand over my flat belly and down to my clit. While I rode him I rubbed myself, each movement the perfect friction.

"Holy shit," he said softly. His eyes were wide, watching while he caressed me.

The look on his face drove me all the way to the edge and over. I let out a soft cry as an orgasm washed over me, deep and intense. My toes curled and my stomach clenched. My pussy tightened around his cock. My head swam, lost in a sea of pure pleasure I could have happily drowned in.

I cried out again, ragged this time.

He matched the sound a moment later with an orgasm of his own. Thrusting up into me, hard and fast while his fingers tightened on my breasts.

"Oh fuck... fuck... Summer." He let out a grunt and sagged back on the bed.

With him still inside me, I lay forward over him and sighed softly.

CHAPTER FIVE

We fucked twice more that night, both times longer and slower than the time before. I snuck out of bed for a quick shower, then snuggled up under his blankets and slept.

The sun was a few hands in the sky before I woke. I lay on my side, Fletcher curled around me, his hand on my hip.

"Morning," he said sleepily.

"Mmm." I nestled in a little deeper. The last few nights were spent on the forest floor, so sleeping in an actual bed was a luxury. One I could get used to.

"I'll bring you some coffee," he whispered. Before I could respond with a, 'hells yes, please,' he slipped out of bed and threw on a pair of track pants.

I drifted back to sleep and woke again to the smell of coffee in front of my nose.

For that, I would get up. Or sit up, anyway.

"Thank you." I accepted the cup and sipped. "I assume Kale hasn't arrived yet?"

Fletcher sat on the side of the bed with his own cup and shook his head. "I haven't seen a sign of him and I didn't hear Tiny. Jude has taken him for a walk, so we'll have to keep watch ourselves."

"Is your *charming* brother awake?" I hadn't had enough coffee to pretend to be nice.

"He's gone to work," Fletcher replied. "We have the place to ourselves."

"Is he always so mean?" I asked bluntly.

He sighed. "He can be difficult, but he's not all bad. We used to be close once."

"What happened?" I asked gently. Maybe I shouldn't be so harsh.

"We got older and grew apart. He was into gaming, cars and girls. I preferred books and dreaming about seeing the world."

"Now you've seen a whole other world," I said.

He inclined his head. "Yes I have." He averted his eyes.

I put a hand on his arm. "What is it? You don't look happy to be home."

He licked his lips. "I am, I just... I *like* the Fae realm. I felt like I belonged there. Here..."

"You wish your brother made you feel more welcome?"

"It's not just that. It's more peaceful there and you, Huon, Kale and Saff, you made me feel like a part of something. Something important. A family, which is trying to save the world. It's like something out of a book."

I smiled. "I suppose it is. And now Jude and Rick are in on it too."

"Where does Jude fit in?" he asked awkwardly.

"I don't know," I admitted. "Not like the rest of you. I think he'll help us, but he's just a friend."

"He has to help us," Fletcher said firmly.

"Oh?" I asked. "Why so?"

He grinned. "Because his car will stay small without you."

I laughed softly. "I would put his car back to normal size even if he didn't help us, but I hope he will. What about Rick?"

"If it helps him in some way," Fletcher said vaguely. "He might not seem like it, but he's a good guy at heart. Deep down. Deep, deep down..." He gave a half smile.

I laughed softly. "If you say he is, then I believe you."

Fletcher finished his coffee and placed the empty cup on the table beside the bed. "He's been angry since our parents died. I don't think he's dealt with it well. I suggested he get help, but..." He shrugged.

"Does that bother you?" I watched him carefully as he mulled over the question in his head.

He opened his mouth and closed it again a couple of times. "I don't like the idea that he might be in pain but won't talk about it. If I bring it up, he changes the subject, or tells me to fuck off."

I snorted a laugh. "I can imagine him doing that."

After a moment Fletcher snorted too. "It's not a big stretch," he agreed. "But if he does that to you again..."

I patted his arm. "I can take care of myself," I replied.

"If I know anything about you, it's that," he assured me. He gave me a soft look, which spoke all the volumes he wasn't ready to say yet.

"I know that about you too," I told him. I took a moment before I added, "When this is over, if you want to stay in the Fae realm...you'd be welcome."

He glanced away, but when he looked back, a tear glinted in his eye. "I think I'd like that," he said softly.

I put down my cup—which wasn't empty—and put my arms around him. "When we fix this and get the veil working again, you can come back here any time."

He leaned into me and nodded against my shoulder. "We have to get it open first."

"Right, and for that we need Kale."

"And breakfast."

"Good point." My stomach rumbled.

He sat back and gave me a quick kiss on my mouth. "I'll make us something."

"I'll get dressed." I realised then he was still shirtless. The fact he felt comfortable enough around me to do that spoke even more words than his eyes did.

"You don't have to," he teased.

I laughed and pushed off the covers to grab my pack and start to pull out clothes. "I think I should. Otherwise people would stare if we left the house."

"Yes, they would," he agreed. "I would be one of those people."

He flashed me a smile, pulled on a shirt and grabbed up our dirty clothes before he headed out the door.

While I dressed, I considered what he said about Rick. We didn't have Fae who listened to other's problems for a living, but I knew how much it helped to talk about them. I also knew, from experience, you couldn't make people talk if they didn't want to.

And then, some folk liked to be angry.

I shrugged on a clean shirt and tucked it into my trousers, then stopped to finish my coffee. Really, I had more important things to worry about right now than Rick, and his issues.

I headed downstairs. "Something smells good."

Fletcher took my mug and placed it upside down in what looked like a cupboard, with a door that opened downward.

I frowned at the contraption.

"It's just toast and that's a dishwasher," he replied. "It's a machine for—"

"Washing dishes?" I finished for him. "I'll say this about humans, you will invent all sorts of machines to avoid doing a few minutes of work."

He grinned. "That's us."

I snorted. "If only you'd invented a machine for making coffee."

"Um…" He looked cagey.

"I should have guessed." I jumped at the sound of toast popping. "I've seen a toaster before," I said while he held back a grin. "I just wasn't ready for it."

"Now you see why I prefer the Fae realm to this," he said.

"Because you get startled by toasters too?" I asked.

He laughed. "Yes, absolutely. Actually, it's all this technology and the need to have the latest of everything."

"We do that too though," I told him. "Clothing goes in and out of style and everyone wants to have the latest dagger."

"A dagger is probably cheaper than a smart-phone," he replied. He pulled out the toast and spread butter on each slice.

"That depends on the dagger," I replied. "But we can't google on them. Yet."

"I hope you never can," he said firmly. "Or should I say *we?*"

"You can say *we*, but until we're sure we can get back, then I'm not even sure what *we* entails."

He grimaced. "Jam?"

"Yes, we will be in one." I sighed.

He stared for a moment, then laughed again. "No, do you want jam on your toast? Or jelly, as the Americans call it."

"Ohhh. I'll have whatever you're having." I waved a hand at the array of jars on the kitchen bench.

"I usually have Vegemite. Maybe you should try it first. It's an acquired taste." He spread some thinly on a piece of toast and handed it to me.

I bit into it. It was salty, but not unpleasant.

I handed the rest of the slice of toast back. "Thank you, it's interesting, but I prefer something sweet."

"At least you didn't spit it out." He held up a finger. "I know, I have just the thing." He opened a jar of something which looked like Vegemite. This time he spread a thick layer on the toast.

I eyed it doubtfully, but bit into it when he passed it to me. My eyes widened. Whatever the spread was, it was sweet and tasted almost as good as coffee.

"It's Nutella," he said.

"I think I'm in love." I sighed.

"Some people eat it straight out of the jar."

"Some people are smart." I finished the toast and reached for the jar and a spoon. While he made coffee, I sat at the table and ate.

"I'm definitely taking some of this back to the Fae realm," I said around the spoon. "I'll need a big bag for all of it and the coffee."

"All the more reason to open the veil." He sat beside me. "You can come back and get more."

I nodded. "And I will—"

I stopped speaking at the sound of music coming from Fletcher's phone. It vibrated so hard it moved a centimetre or two across the table.

"It's a movie theme song." He reached for the phone just before it fell off onto the floor. "One of my favourite sci-fi ones."

I gave him a blank look. I'd seen movies, but I had no idea which one this tune was from.

"We'll have to watch before we go back." He pressed the screen and put the phone to his ear.

"Hello? Yes, this is… Oh, really? He does?" He glanced at me.

I gave him a questioning look in return, but he only shook his head.

"Yes. Yes, we'll be right down there." He pressed the screen again and put the phone down.

"It seems we've found Saff. Or he's found us."

I blinked in surprise. Of all the guys, his was the name I least expected to hear. I didn't know why. He was just as smart and resourceful as the others.

"Where is he? Is Huon with him?"

"Down at the police station," Fletcher replied. "It seems he walked straight in the door and asked if they knew how to find me. They didn't mention anyone else."

"Evidently they did know where to find you," I remarked.

"Yes, but I'm surprised they humoured him. Usually they have better things to do than track people down. Unless they're criminals, which I'm not." He finished his last piece of toast and washed it down with coffee.

"It's Saff. I'm surprised he didn't get them to drive him here." I rose and put my mug and spoon in the dishwasher. The rest of the Nutella, I'd save for later.

Fletcher smiled, but he glanced toward the door. "Should one of us wait and see if Kale turns up?"

"Don't worry, we can do that," Khat remarked as he slinked into the kitchen, Tiny and Jude on his heels.

"Where have you been?" I asked the mimicat.

"Out and about," he replied. He jumped onto the couch and curled up in a ball. He placed his head on his paws, closed his eyes and looked as though he went asleep straight away.

It seemed that was all the answer I was going to get.

I shrugged and smiled at Jude. "Morning. Do you mind waiting here for Kale or Huon?" It seemed they hadn't all found their way to the human realm together. If Saff had the sense to find Fletcher, surely Huon would as well?

"You're welcome to use the wifi," Fletcher said. "The password is on the fridge. The TV has all the streaming services. Maybe stay away from the Nutella, but otherwise help yourself to whatever you can find."

Jude nodded. "I don't mind, but I might need my car back when you've brought your friend back."

"Oh yes." I had forgotten about his car. "We won't be long. I hope," I added under my voice. I gave the dog a pat before he jumped beside Khat and proceeded to drool on the couch.

Fletcher grimaced but led the way out the door.

CHAPTER SIX

When we arrived at the police station, Saff looked to have made himself at home. He sat with his eyes closed, on a chair to the side of a waiting area, his legs stretched out across two more. He rested his back against the wall.

At first I thought he was asleep. His eyes popped open as soon as we approached and he grinned.

"Summer, Fletcher, it's good to see you two." He stretched slowly and sat up.

"This man is with you?" a woman in a blue uniform called out from behind a desk at the end of the room. Her hair was done up in a tight bun and she wore an expression to match.

"Well..." I started. A smile tugged at the corners of my mouth.

"Hey," Saff protested.

I smiled. "Yes, he's with us. I hope he didn't give you too much trouble."

The officer's expression was unchanged. "Just get him out of here. Make sure he doesn't need to be brought back."

"We'll see to it," Fletcher assured her.

She nodded. Her eyes lingered on his scars before she looked back toward the papers in front of her.

I exchanged a look with Saff and he shrugged.

It wasn't until we were back outside before he said, "I was nothing but polite."

I eyed him doubtfully.

He held up both hands, palms forward. "I promise. I might have used a little magic, but that was—"

"Are you crazy?" I rounded on him. "We're supposed to keep a low profile here."

"I was trying to find you." He walked with his eyes down for a moment. "Ever since I almost drowned, I've felt this… I don't know… connection to you. Kale says the key pulled him in the direction it wanted him to go, right?"

I nodded. "That is what he said, yes."

"Well, I feel like I'm being pulled toward you in the same way. I tried to use magic to enhance it, but —" He swallowed audibly.

"You didn't hurt anyone, did you?" Fletcher asked.

"No!" Saff replied. "But it turns out I can attract all the butterflies within a several kilometre radius."

"Butterflies?" I frowned.

"I might have been thinking pretty, colourful and with wings," Saff explained. "Turns out, that police officer in there has a phobia. She chased them all away with a wad of paper. I thought she was going to pee herself. She couldn't exactly blame me, but I think she knew I did something."

"Attracting butterflies," Fletcher mused. "No offence, but that might be the most useless magic trick I've ever heard of."

"No offence taken," Saff said lightly. "Unless they could pick me up and fly me to you, it *is* useless."

I frowned. "I hope that's not some peculiar part to this whole puzzle."

"You think that's what this is?" Fletcher asked. "Another puzzle?"

I ran a hand over my hair. "I feel as though this whole thing is just that. We have to find all the pieces and put them in place. Speaking of pieces, have you seen Kale and Huon?"

Saff's face fell. "They're not with you?"

I shook my head. "With any luck, they'll feel the same draw."

"With any luck, Kale has found the second key," Fletcher remarked.

I sighed. "You're right. Whatever we do, we need to find him." I looked toward Saff. "You haven't felt drawn to Kale?"

"I'm very drawn to him," Saff said cheerfully. "I'd happily let him fuck my—" He saw my expression and stopped. "But no, not like that. I could try magic again, but—"

"No," Fletcher and I said at the same time.

"I think we've drawn enough attention to ourselves without being surrounded by a swarm of butterflies."

"It could have been worse," Saff remarked.

"Yes," Fletcher agreed, "you could have attracted a swarm of hipsters."

I gave him a funny look, but shrugged. "I'm not sure if we should try looking for Kale and Huon, or the key." Doing both was an option, but not one I favoured. We'd only been separated for a matter of hours, but that was more than enough. I didn't want to risk losing either of them again.

"They have to be around here somewhere," Saff said. "If the veil dropped us in the same country, then it makes sense it did the same with us all."

I nodded slowly. "They might be nearby some-where. How big is Australia?"

"Big," Fletcher replied. "We can't just walk around and find them."

I sighed. I figured out that last bit already. "All right, maybe we could go back to your place and try some magic. No one will notice a bunch of insects there."

"Especially if you blow them up," Saff teased.

I sniffed. "I don't blow *everything* up."

"Just bugs and mountains," Flynn said.

"And rose petals." That seemed like another life-time ago now. "Saff, what would Huon do to find us?"

Saff rubbed his chin. "He would… he'd probably sit tight and hope we find him."

I sighed because he was right.

"Where did you come out?" Fletcher asked suddenly.

"Just over there." Saff pointed to a park about fifty metres down at the end of the street.

"Bell's Hill," I replied. "Why?"

Fletcher pulled out his phone. "Because I was exactly twenty kilometres from you. And you were twenty kilometres from Saff." He blinked. "If this was the centre point, I was due east and you were south."

"So Kale and Huon might be west and north of here, respectively," I said slowly. "I suppose it's possible."

"It gives us somewhere to start," Saff said.

"Right," Fletcher agreed, "but I need something bigger than my phone to figure out where to look. We'll need to go home and use my computer."

"You don't have a paper map?" I asked.

"I… they do still exist," Fletcher said. "I should have one at home somewhere. It might be a little out of date, but it should do,"

"Back to your place then," I said. Before any of us could go anywhere, I grabbed Saff's hand, drew him to me and pressed my mouth to his.

"I'm glad you're safe," I told him.

He wound an arm around my waist and kissed me back. "Me too," he replied. He grinned and added. "I'm glad you're safe as well."

I socked him lightly on the arm. While he rubbed it, I said, "Don't make us regret coming down here to get you."

"I would never make you regret coming," he said.

I glanced at Fletcher. "Six?"

He looked bemused. "I think it's closer to a seven."

"You two are harsh." Saff pouted. "It was at least an eight."

I grinned. "Come on, let's go. The sooner we work out where we have to go, the sooner we can get there."

"As long as we can stop long enough for me to eat," Saff said. "I'm starving."

"The police didn't feed you?" I asked playfully.

"Not even a cup of coffee." He sighed dramatically.

"Don't you have laws about depriving people of caffeine?" I asked Fletcher.

"Surprisingly, no," he replied. "People are even expected to be responsible for their own behaviour when they haven't had a cup recently." His eyes shone with amusement.

"That's barbaric." I shook my head.

"Isn't it though?' He shrugged and clicked the button on the key to unlock the car.

I climbed in beside him and Saff tumbled into the back seat.

"You didn't fly here?"

"Remember the bit about being inconspicuous?" I asked over my shoulder.

"Remember how we can become smaller than the butterflies?" he retorted.

"Maybe you should have had one give you a ride," Fletcher quipped.

"Hey, good idea. I'll have to keep that in mind for next time." Saff sat back and clicked his seatbelt.

I pictured him riding on the back of one and snorted. It wasn't that big a stretch to imagine him doing something so ridiculous, but it wasn't something I would try. I preferred to fly under my own power, or walk.

That led to another question though. I twisted around in my seat to ask, "Did you call them to you, or did you try to get them to do anything?"

He frowned. "It didn't occur to me to ask. I was too busy watching the police officer chase them away. Why?"

"I don't know." I sat back around. "It's probably not important."

"You must have asked for a reason," Fletcher said gently. "Do you think it's another piece of the puzzle?"

"I don't know," I admitted. "I've never heard of a Fae attracting insects or having a magical bond with another Fae. That it's happening now can't be a coincidence."

"Well, it can," Saff drawled, "but it probably isn't.

Do you think I'm supposed to call down hordes of creepy crawlies to find the second key?"

I shuddered. "I hope not." I leaned back against the seat and closed my eyes. I'd have to mull it over and keep an eye out. Although—it might be nothing. This whole situation might be making me see things which weren't really there.

On the other hand, an anchor washed up on a remote beach in the Fae realm did get us here. The gods only knew what other random things were actually important. We couldn't rule out anything at this stage.

"How does the bond feel now you're closer to Summer?" Fletcher asked.

I thought maybe he was asking out of jealousy, but I saw his expression. He merely looked curious. Thank the gods for that. We had enough on our plates without anyone's envy getting in the way.

"It feels..." Saff paused. "It feels comfortable. Like a satisfied itch. Mostly. Being near her makes me horny as all hells."

I smiled and shook my head. "Aren't you like that most of the time anyway?"

"True," he said cheerfully. "I am."

"Why do you talk about hells and gods, plural?" Fletcher drew the car to a stop at the lights.

"Because only god would be lonely," I replied. "We believe in seven of them, and seven hells to match. One for the head, one for the heart, one for the soul, one for redemption."

"One for sex," Saff interjected.

"Originally they were specifically for reproduction," I said. "Although since so much sex won't or can't result in children, their use became broader."

"LGTBA god," Fletcher remarked. "I like it. It's nice to know Fae are tolerant."

"We're nothing if not accepting of the way others live," I replied. "The god associated with the heart used to be solely for women and the head was for men. Since that made no sense, it's changed."

"The last two are for the irredeemable and resurrection. The hells aren't bad places, just a state the soul lingers in before rebirth."

"Unless you're irredeemable," Saff said. "Then your soul might stay there forever and suffer."

"That's only for the worst of the worst," I said.

"What does that include?" Fletcher steered through the traffic as the light turned green. He slammed on the brakes and swore as a white Jeep swerved in front and cut us off. They missed hitting Fletcher's car a hair.

"Driving like that?" Fletcher suggested. He pressed the horn. The sound made me jump.

The Jeep's driver gave us a rude gesture with her finger and sped off.

I grimaced. My heart pounded from the near miss. "Only if someone had died," I replied.

"They might if she drives like that," Fletcher said dryly. "Funny, her car looks familiar..." He shook it off and turned down the street to his house.

"No offence, but I think I prefer to fly," I said as I took my seatbelt off.

"Even when we're chased by giant birds or beetles?" Fletcher asked.

"Good point." I shut the door behind me and headed inside.

CHAPTER SEVEN

*T*iny didn't seem to have moved in our absence. He wagged his tail as we entered, thumping it against the couch several times.

"Stop that, you overgrown mutt." Khat's tail flicked this way and that in irritation.

Tiny thumped harder a few more times, then lay still.

Jude sat on the other side of the dog, his feet propped up on the coffee table. He made himself a sandwich and a cup of tea, judging by the label which dangled from the cup by a piece of string. The TV was on and what looked like drawn, yellow people moved across the screen.

"Well hello there." Saff stepped over and flopped

down beside Jude. "I'm Saff, who might you be?" He held out his hand.

Jude shook it. He looked at Saff as though he couldn't quite believe what he was seeing. "I'm Jude. This is Tiny." He nodded toward the dog.

Saff smiled. "Charmed. What are we watching?" He snuggled down next to Jude and looked very cozy.

"An animated show," Jude replied. "That's…" He started to explain while Saff nodded, enraptured.

I exchanged glances and shrugs with Fletcher.

"I'll get the map," he said.

"I'll make some hot chocolate," I replied.

He gave me a funny look.

"What? A girl can't just live on coffee."

"Uh, true enough." Fletcher headed toward the stairs.

I headed into the kitchen and made sandwiches —Nutella for me, Vegemite for Saff—and boiled the electric kettle.

Just as it clicked off, Fletcher trotted down the stairs and spread a map across the dining table.

He rubbed the creases where the paper had been folded. "This is where we are." He drew a circle around the place with a black pen.

Jude appeared over his shoulder and pointed.

"That's my house there. I met Summer on the street outside."

"And me," Khat said, one eye open and fixed on us.

"And him," Jude agreed.

"Here's where Saff came out." Fletcher drew a X on a section of green. "Now, I need—" He straightened up and looked around the room.

"Ah, this will do." He grabbed a hardcover book from a bookshelf and carried it to the table. He lay it down on the map, with the cover open, and traced a line between each location.

"West is about where they're building a new airport," he said slowly. He squinted at the map and rubbed his chin.

"Shit."

"What?" I asked. I followed his gaze. "Oh. Is that blue what I think it is?"

"Unfortunately, yes. It's in the middle of the harbour."

"Lucky they have wings." Saff all but put his chin on Fletcher's shoulder to peer over it.

"Yes, but they couldn't stay put if they ended up there," I replied. "They'd have to get to land eventually."

"The closest land to it then," Fletcher ran a finger across the map, "is Darling Harbour."

"Yes, darling?" Saff batted his eyelashes.

Fletcher rolled his eyes. "That's what it's called; Darling Harbour."

"I know," Saff replied. "I can read."

"Do you want to sock him or should I?" I said to Fletcher.

"Be my guest." Fletcher waved a hand toward Saff.

I socked him lightly on the arm.

"Ouch," he said, his expression deadpan. "Aren't there laws against that?"

"Only if someone saw it," Fletcher said. "I didn't see anything. Did you Jude?"

"Not a thing," Jude replied.

"Me either. Now be quiet, I'm trying to sleep," Khat snapped.

"You could give us some help instead," I told him. He probably heard me, but didn't respond. I shook my head and pointed at the X on the western part of the map.

"I guess we start there then."

Fletcher nodded. "If one is at Darling Harbour, they'd be less noticeable, even if they walked around with their wings out."

Jude laughed. "That's true. It can get flamboyant down there, especially this close to the pride parade."

"Pride?" I asked.

"Right. It's a parade for LGTBA-plus folk to celebrate being fabulous."

"I celebrate that daily," Saff said.

"Yes, you do, don't you?" I agreed.

"What's not to celebrate?" Saff shrugged.

"Not everyone in the human world is nice about it," Jude said softly.

Saff patted his arm. "You have us now. We accept you, whatever your orientation." He gave Jude a questioning look.

"I'm gay," Jude muttered.

"Excellent!" Saff declared. "See, that was easy, wasn't it?"

Jude smiled tentatively. "Are all Fae like this?"

"No," Saff replied, "Huon is an ass. Don't worry though, his heart is in the right place. Mostly."

I shook my head. "Ignore him. He and Huon love to give each other a hard time. And that's *not* an innuendo. As far as I know…"

Saff shook his head. "Huon only has eyes for the pretty girls."

"And Summer," Khat said from his spot on the couch.

"Fuck off," I told him. "Do you *want* me to let Tiny eat you?"

"First the troll, now the dog," Khat complained. "Why does everyone want to eat me?" He cracked open an eye.

I regarded all three guys, but none said a word.

I shook my head. "That was far too obvious, wasn't it?"

"I wouldn't think you'd give us a high number," Fletcher replied. "There's no subtlety in 'eating pussy' jokes."

I nodded slowly. "You're right. I would have given a two. Three at the most."

"You folk are a riot," Khat said sarcastically.

"What we are is in a hurry," I said. I downed the rest of my hot chocolate, which was only warm by now, and grabbed my sandwich. "Jude, where is your car?"

He pulled it out of his pocket and handed it to me. "Do you want me to drive?"

"Your car is bigger," I replied, "but if you don't want to be involved anymore…"

"I don't mind," he said quickly. "I was involved the moment we met and your friend over there talked." He waved toward Khat.

"I'm not sure I'd call him a friend," I said dryly. In spite of that, I added, "Khat, are you coming?"

He yawned and stretched. "I might as well. I'm getting bored."

"Still haven't found your mate?" I guessed that was what he was doing out last night.

His flinch confirmed my suspicions.

"No," he said, grumpier than usual. "Not a sign. The cats around here are useless. Meow this, meow that, not a clue between them."

"They don't speak human?" I asked.

"Oh they do, they just have nothing to say. It's all mice, sunshine and their favourite brand of cat food. Even the cat in heat—"

"Khat," I said sharply, "did you cheat on your mate?"

"We have an open relationship," he replied tersely.

"Are you sure those kittens are yours?" Saff asked.

"Do you want me to bite you on the dick?" Khat growled.

Saff looked thoughtful. "Well—"

I cleared my throat. "We really don't have time for this."

Without waiting any further, I walked out the front door. I crouched down, placed Jude's car on the street and made it back to its normal size.

"What the hell?" a voice exclaimed.

A woman with white hair and a face full of wrinkles, stepped toward me, her eyes full of suspicion and confusion.

"How'd you do that?" she demanded.

"Do what?" I asked. I smiled and tried to look innocent.

She rubbed her eyes. "There was no car, then there was a car."

Fletcher stepped up beside me. "It just pulled up," he said.

"Ain't no one driving." She pointed a shaky finger at the vehicle.

"Self-driving cars," Fletcher said with a nod. "The future is now."

"Not ones that pop up out of nowhere," she said insistently. She tottered forward on thin legs and touched the car as if it might disappear.

"See, it's a perfectly ordinary car." Jude pressed the button to unlock it and opened the back door. Tiny leapt in and stretched out on the seat. "You might have to squash up a bit."

Khat jumped in after the dog and sat between his front paws.

"What the hell are you folks?" the woman asked. "Since when do cats and dogs behave like that?"

"Since they felt like it," Khat replied.

The woman's eyes rolled back in her head and Fletcher and Saff just managed to catch her before she fell to the ground in a faint.

"Did you *have* to talk?" I asked him.

"Yes," he replied. "Yes I did."

I sighed and rubbed my forehead with my finger-tips. "What are we supposed to do with her now?"

"We could take her over to the grass and leave her there?" Saff suggested.

"We can't do that! The gods know what might happen to her," I protested.

"I know who she is," Fletcher said. "She lives three doors down. We'll take her home."

I wanted to grind my teeth. We'd wasted enough time as it was. "All right, let's do that."

Saff and Fletcher lifted the woman into Fletcher's arms. He staggered forward under her weight.

Her house was the same size as Fletcher's, but run down and unkempt. Weeds grew through cracks on the top of the front steps and around the sides. Seeing them reminded me of why we were here. Even though they were unwanted plants, they were healthier than many of the trees in the Fae realm. Had they gotten worse in our absence? Had the taint spread closer to the Fae capital?

I hated the idea of the beautiful trees we made our homes in, rotting and smelling so deeply of death and decay. The Fae would eventually die.

I climbed the steps and pressed the doorbell. I didn't hear it ring, so I rapped on the screen door with my knuckles.

The knock was followed by the sound of slow, heavy footsteps. The door swung open and a face as wrinkled as the woman's peered at me from behind the screen door. The man's eyes were a brilliant blue and full of undisguised contempt.

"We don't want any," he said. "Go away." The door was slammed in my face before I could even open my mouth.

I grumbled under my breath and knocked again.

The door opened a second time. "I said we don't want—" He stopped and peered around me.

"Myrtle?" He squinted. "What've you gone and done to Myrtle?" He rattled the screen door unlocked and opened it. It creaked as though it hadn't opened in years.

"We didn't do anything, sir," Fletcher said, his tone polite. "She seems to have fainted. We just brought her back—"

"Is she dead?" the man snapped.

"No," Fletcher said quickly. "She just—"

"Shame." The man clicked his tongue. "You better bring her in." He backed up a few steps and moved aside.

Fletcher gave me a look, his brow creased.

I shrugged. Not everyone had a happy relationship, but I couldn't imagine wanting anyone to die, not even Khat when he was being his usual, grumpy self.

Fletcher turned sideways and shuffled inside carefully, taking each step at a time.

"Mind the doorframe," the man said bluntly. "Myrtle's head is hard."

"Are you always so nice to your wife?" I asked sarcastically.

The man burst out laughing. "She's not my wife. The old bitch is my sister." He muttered to himself and shook his head.

Fletcher grimaced. I saw him thinking he could relate to this man on some level. He lowered Myrtle to the couch as she started to stir.

"There you are," he said awkwardly and stepped back. "We'll go and get out of your hair then."

"What hair?" The man patted his shining head and barked a bitter laugh. "I ain't had hair since 1996. Overrated if you ask me."

"Right." Fletcher stepped toward the door. I followed him.

"Leaving so soon?" Myrtle sat up. She fixed me with a firm look and her face began to change.

"We've been expecting you."

CHAPTER EIGHT

hat the fuck?

"What are you?" I asked, wary.

The elderly, wrinkled face was gone, replaced by smooth skin, clear eyes and long, blonde hair. She looked like me. No, me with a sprinkle of Tavar.

"I'm Myrta." Her voice was strong and deep, with an accent that tugged at the back of my memory. "I am one of the ancients. We have been waiting since the days of the trullen."

Tavar told us about the trullen, Fae born without wings. The ancestors of the trolls. And the Risi, which were the ancestors of Fae and trolls.

"That was a thousand years ago. Not even Fae live that long," I pointed out.

"Time moves differently here," Myrta said as

though I were a child. "More slowly. However—" She swung her legs over and rose from the couch. She stood a head taller than me. If she was trying to intimidate me, she succeeded.

I held my ground but my tongue darted over my lips.

She seemed amused by this. "The devallan are longer lived than modern Fae." She sniffed as though we were lesser beings of some kind.

I eyed her for a moment, then looked over to her brother. He had also changed. He now had long, dark hair and pale skin. While no longer the decrepit human, he still looked unwell, tired.

"Let me guess, you're the last two of your kind?" I addressed Myrta directly.

When she flinched, I knew I was right.

"Cyrir and I have lived for long enough to do the job we were put here for," Myrta stated proudly.

Cyrir looked as though he might be knocked over by a stray breeze, but Myrta seemed strong enough.

"And what is that?" I asked, my hand on my hip. My tough Fae act was just that, an act. However old they might be, they were powerful. I felt magic waft around them like too much perfume.

"To stop you," Myrta said.

"Ah, I see." I glanced at Fletcher. He looked as anxious as I felt. "Nothing says stealthy like announcing your intentions."

"Stealth got you into this building," Cyrir pointed out.

"Saff was right," I said to Fletcher. "We should have left her lying on the grass out there."

He nodded. "I'm sorry. Helping her was my idea."

I patted his arm. "It's all right. It's always good to be nice."

He shrugged. "I suppose so."

"It is, believe me," I assured him. I turned back to Myrta. "Since we're being so open about things, you might as well tell me why you want to stop us. The Fae realm is dying. Personally, that's not what I prefer to have happen."

"The Fae realm is, and always was, diseased," Myrta hissed. "The trolls are proof of this."

"The trolls were created by a faction of Risi—" I started.

"The nympha," Myrta said. "I know. I was there. At the dawn of time. At the dawn of everything."

"She's exaggerating slightly," Cyrir said. "We were there when the nympha were put on trial for creating the trullen. We were there when the elders took the dark magic from the nympha and spread the keys across the worlds. We were there when the nympha were exiled."

"That's what you are," Fletcher said suddenly. "You're nympha in exile."

I clapped a hand to my forehead. Why hadn't I seen it sooner? Their ability to change their faces was a magic I'd never heard of. That kind of deception couldn't be benign.

"You used dark magic, but most of it was taken when you were exiled here," I guessed. "Otherwise you would have killed us already."

"I could still use a knife," Myrta said dryly.

"No, you can't, or you would have done that too." I shook my head. "You want the Fae realm to die. Why?"

"Like I said, it's—"

"Diseased. Yes, yes." I waved my hand. "The human realm isn't precisely well either."

"You have a god of rebirth," Fletcher said softly.

I turned my head toward him slightly. "Yes, we do."

"That's what they want," he said. "They want the worlds to die and be reborn. They want to be at the dawn of time."

"Genocide," I whispered. "On such a scale…"

"The gods would tremble," Myrta said proudly. "They will fall at our feet and beg to worship us."

"Like all genocidal maniacs, you're insane," Fletcher said.

"Do you know many genocidal maniacs?" I asked curiously.

"I know *of* some," he replied. "Human history is littered with them. Hitler, Stalin, some of the world's present leaders…"

"Ah, I see." I nodded. I turned back to Myrta. "So here's what I'm guessing. When you were exiled here, you were put under a magic thrall of some kind, which prevents you from actually harming anyone. Am I right?"

"In a manner of speaking." She stepped closer to me. "While I can't hurt anyone, you can."

I scratched my head. "I don't want to though. So far, nothing you've said has convinced me to stop doing what we're doing. Sorry, it looks as though we've wasted your time. I held out a hand. "Come on Fletcher, let's go. We've wasted our own time here as well."

"You're a fool," Myrta said scathingly. "You have no idea what you're dealing with."

"A bored old lady with nothing but idle death threats?" I guessed.

She bared her teeth and advanced on me.

I held my ground, but sweat broke out under my arms and on my palms. Even if she couldn't cause me injury, the magic which surrounded her was still more powerful than I could ever have dreamed of.

"Nothing I do is idle," she growled.

Without meaning to, I shrank back, but she grabbed my hand.

Magic surged into me like the wave which had swept Saff under. It washed over me, swamped my mind, my body. Darkness shrouded me, pressing it hard, too hard. My vision blurred, swam. I blinked but it wouldn't clear.

I couldn't breathe. My knees weakened, barely able to hold me up.

Only her hand on mine kept me on my feet.

"Stop," I gasped out. "Enough... please..."

"Surrender," she insisted.

"No... I... " My mind was in a fog. Thoughts jumbled and clogged, confused. Nothing made sense.

Then suddenly, everything cleared in a silent snap. I caught a breath, but it felt strange, like I was watching, feeling from a distance.

My hand appeared in front of my face, but I hadn't moved it. The laugh which emerged from between my lips wasn't mine. The form Myrta had taken was gone.

Her soul was inside me now.

I screamed, but no sound came out.

I watched in horror as Cyrir approached Fletcher. He reached his hand out toward him.

Fletcher ducked away. He looked around and picked up a chair.

Another laugh escaped my lips. I tried to push it down, to deny Myrta control of my body. It slipped out anyway.

No, no no!

"You can't escape, human," Myrta taunted.

I batted against her, shouted at her, shouted at Fletcher to run.

"I can hear you, little Fae," she said out loud. I had no doubt she was talking to me.

You bitch! Get out of my head.

She chuckled. "I'm not going anywhere. Except to find the second key. When we have them all, we'll have our dark magic back."

You want what we want, I reasoned, *the keys. Why not let us get them for you?*

"Because you wouldn't give them to me when you

have them," she replied. "Or the implements of dark magic when you find them."

What would I do with dark magic? I just want to free lesser magic and stop it from screwing up the Fae realm.

"The Fae realm is breathing its last breaths," Myrta said scathingly. "Even if you return lesser magic, you won't succeed."

You're a little ray of fucking sunshine, you know that?

Fletcher was still fending off Cyrir with the chair, but the ancient nympha only looked amused.

"Summer?"

I'm in here! I knew he couldn't hear me, but I shouted anyway.

Myrta laughed. She stepped toward Fletcher. "It's beneath us to inhabit another human, but you have no choice. Your Fae lover is happy with me inside her mind."

Lying bitch, I hissed.

Fletcher glanced toward me. "I doubt that," he said evenly. "The people who lived here, when did you steal their bodies?"

I gasped. It should have occurred to me this wasn't the first time they'd done this, but it hadn't. The implications of that... I had to push it away. Whatever I thought, Myrta would know.

Myrta laughed. "We've only been here since you

came through the portal. We felt you, knew you'd come here. If not for you, they would still be living out their final years."

I snorted, or thought about snorting. *Whatever you did to them is on you, not me.* Something occurred to me. Are there *three of you? Is Rick an evil nympha too?*

"Hells no, he's just an asshole," she replied.

Figures.

"That's my brother you're talking about," Fletcher growled. He must have put two and two together and figured who was being talked about.

Cyrir lunged at him, but he brought the chair up again.

"I guess your magic sucks, or you would have just used it," Fletcher remarked.

"Good point." Myrta raised her hand.

Fletcher!

A blast of magic hit the wall behind Fletcher. It sent wood and plaster into the air.

He dropped the chair and threw his hands over his face.

I thought he was done, but Cyrir also covered his eyes against the spray of debris.

"Watch it!" he growled. "I need me *and* this human alive."

Myrta smiled. "I could do this alone."

We have friends. If Fletcher doesn't leave this house, they'll come looking.

"Do you think I'm scared, little Fae?" she asked. Still, she lowered her hand. "Hurry up, you old fool. He's only a human. He shouldn't be a match for a one-thousand-year-old nympha."

Oh, you have no idea, I told her. *He's more than a match for you both.*

"Does he have magic?" When I didn't respond, she laughed. "He is nothing, just as you are."

I sat back in my own mind and pouted.

Cyrir grabbed Fletcher's arm and turned into a mist before he disappeared into the body of my lover.

All I could do was watch and cry.

"That's better." Fletcher wiped his hands on his jean legs. "He's no Fae, but it's an improvement on the old man." He rolled his shoulders and his head and nodded. "Yes, he'll do nicely."

Fletcher! He couldn't hear me, but I felt as though he turned his eyes toward me and screamed out to me. I tried to do the same, but Myrta turned my face away from him.

"Now, now, none of that. Don't worry, you'll soon lose the connection to your former bodies soon enough. When that happens, you'll fade away and cease to exist."

Excuse me if that doesn't sound like fun. I had to hold on as long as I could and find a way to get her out of me. Assuming that was even possible. If I had to die to rid both realms of her, then so be it. Kale, Huon and Saff could carry on without me.

"It will be fun. Then I'll have this cute body for another thousand years. And all your lovers too." She pinched my nipples which would have hurt if she hadn't shoved me to the back of my mind. As it was, I flinched and winced. If it hurt her, she showed no sign. Maybe she liked pain, or just wanted to feel alive.

You're right about one thing, I said dryly, *I am cute. But it's my body and I'll get it back or die trying.*

"So dramatic," she scolded. "Now shut up, I have work to do. Cyrir, it's time to join their friends on the next step of their journey." She offered him her arm.

He gave her a slight frown, but took it. Either he didn't like their plan, or he didn't like her. It didn't matter, if I could exploit the rift between them, maybe I could find a way out of here.

We stepped back outside, and down the cracked front steps.

The sound of Cyrir closing the door behind us sounded horribly final.

CHAPTER NINE

"*F*letcher, you sit in the back." Myrta was quick to organise everyone and slide into the passenger seat beside Jude.

Has anyone told you you're bossy? I asked.

She ignored me and looked over to the backseat of the car.

Khat rose and arched his back the moment Cyrir opened the door to climb inside. He hissed.

"Is there a problem, *cat*?" Myrta asked. "Maybe we should leave you behind."

Saff looked surprised. "I know you two don't get along, but didn't you say you thought we should all stay together?"

"Of course I did," Myrta said smoothly, "but his attitude is tiresome."

"Tiresome?" Saff mouthed. "I know he can be difficult—"

"What are you?" Khat growled.

Saff and Jude both looked perplexed. Of course, leave it to Khat to be the only one to know anything was up.

"I'm a Fae," Myrta said, as though he was a small child. "I'm sure you've seen my kind before."

Khat's tail flicked and even Tiny began to growl. "No one has seen your kind for a long, long time."

"Have you had too much catnip?" Myrta asked. "Come along now, we're wasting time. Leave the cat here if he's going to be troublesome."

Saff looked from me to Khat, clearly confused. "Khat, it's just Summer and Fletcher. What is your problem?"

Khat sniffed. "It's them, but... it's not. Can't you feel the malevolence?"

"The only thing I feel is impatience," Saff replied. "We need to find Huon and Kale, and the key."

"Precisely," Myrta said with a nod. "Now get out or shut up."

Khat's tail flicked another time or two, then he lay back down. He kept his eyes open until Myrta turned away and I could no longer see what he was doing. I hoped to the gods he would keep pushing, but not to the point where Myrta caused him harm. Maybe when we found Kale and Huon, Khat could convince them to help me.

Saff shrugged and slid in beside Khat and Fletcher. Tiny took up so much room so they were squashed in, but Saff looked content.

"So, you know where we're going?" Jude asked Fletcher.

"Yes, the place on the map," Cyrir replied stiffly.

If anyone else noticed, no one said anything. I wanted to scream at them. Instead I sat back and tried to figure out if somehow I could access my magic. Maybe if I could...

Myrta tapped my forehead. "No, no, none of that," she said softly.

"Did you say something?" Jude asked.

"Not a thing," Myrta replied easily. "Off we go then."

Keep talking like that, I told her sarcastically, *they won't suspect a thing.*

When she didn't reply, I chuckled.

What's wrong, can't respond unless you speak out loud? Great, that means I can chat and you'll just have to listen.

Even without words, the way she stiffened—I suppose it was our body for the moment—showed her annoyance. That was heartening. Maybe I would bother her into leaving. I didn't want to inflict her on someone else, but I wanted her out of me.

Whatever you're up to, you won't win. I see you have access to my memories. That being the case, you know we've already done whatever we've needed to do to get this far. We will do whatever it takes to save the Fae realm and the human realm from you, and any more like you.

I felt her stifle a laugh. *There aren't more like you, are there?* I asked. *Good, then we just have to get rid of you two.*

"Jude," Myrta asked," have you got a piece of paper and a pen in the car?"

"Yeah, in there." Jude waved a hand at the glovebox.

She opened it, rummaged through and found both. On the sheet of paper, she wrote, *If you don't be quiet, I will kill Saff and your pet human. Both are dispensable.*

Bitch, I muttered. *Neither are dispensable, especially Saff. And if you do anything to Jude, he'll crash the car and we'll all die. On the other hand, maybe that would be all right. At least you and your dear brother will be dead.*

She wrote again. *Last chance.*

Lucky for you, I have nothing else to say. If I could, I would have crossed my arms and pouted.

She scrunched up the paper and tossed it out the gap in the window.

"Summer, don't be a litterbug." Saff sounded amused.

"Oops." Myrta laughed. "I suppose that was a dumb thing to do. But then again, it's me."

I added an eye roll to the list of things I would do if I could.

Saff laughed, which put him on my shit list, albeit well under Myrta and Cyrir. Did he really see me like that?

"Your recklessness is a part of your charm," Saff said, "but I think I've seen enough of the police already today."

"You're right," Myrta giggled. "You've seen enough of *them* and not enough of *me*."

I do not *talk like that,* I protested.

Myrta swivelled around and I saw Saff grin.

"I could never see enough of you," he said.

"If you don't stop that, I *will* puke on you," Khat said darkly. "That's not Summer. You're flirting with a demon."

Saff frowned at him. "I really don't understand why you're being mean to her all of a sudden."

"I don't understand why you're seeing her with

your cock instead of your brain," Khat replied scathingly. "Or your magic."

Saff looked taken aback, then thoughtful. After a while, he shook his head. "My magic drew me to her and it still is. That's just Summer."

"It's Summer," Khat agreed, "but it's not *just* Summer."

"Fletcher, dear," Myrta said, "perhaps you can wind down your window and throw the mimicat out of it for me."

Saff laughed. "No need for that. Khat will behave. Won't you, Khat?" He gave the mimicat a meaningful look.

"When this is over, I *will* say I told you so," Khat grumbled.

I didn't blame him, he was trying. Nor did I blame Saff. For a moment, I had hoped his magic would reveal the truth. What was the point of magic if it couldn't lead us in the right direction, and do what we need it to? I felt as though something or someone was guiding us, something to do with magic. It seemed as though we were on our own now though.

Silence fell over us for a long while after that. I tried not to think too much, since Myrta would know. I tried to peer into her thoughts, but wherever in my head they were, they were blocked off from me.

After that, I found it harder to focus on my thoughts, so I stopped trying. If that kind of effort would speed up the process of my soul slipping away, then I had no choice. I needed to hang on until I could get out.

I wanted to look back at Fletcher, who must be as scared as I was, but Myrta didn't turn until Jude stopped the car on a quiet road on the other side of the city.

"You think one of them ended up here?" Saff asked.

"It's what the map said, isn't it?" Fletcher-Cyrir snapped.

Saff stepped back, hands in the air. "Steady, buddy. I suppose that's what it said. That was what you told us anyway."

He glanced toward Khat. "I think you have a point. Fletcher and Summer are acting weird."

"We're just eager to save the Fae realm, that's all," Myrta said. "Is there anything wrong with that?"

"No, of course not," Saff replied quickly. "I get it, you're both on edge."

"Exactly," Myrta replied. She smiled sweetly and

added, "And we're both so tired. We were up most of the night, rutting."

Rutting? Who uses words like that anymore? At least I could see Fletcher's face now. His eyes were snapping with anger. It wasn't Cyrir, I was sure of it. Somehow Fletcher was fighting back with more success than I'd had so far. It gave me a surge of hope.

"So, Saff..." Myrta sidled up to him and put an arm around him. "Is your magic telling you who we're here to find and if they're close?"

"I sense something important, but not who. Maybe it's the key."

Myrta smiled broadly. "Excellent. Can you tell where?"

He lowered his arm and moved a few steps away. He turned around slowly, eyes closed, face scrunched up in focus. Eventually he stopped and pointed toward a field full of large vehicles. None of which was moving.

"Earth clearing equipment," Jude said. "If your key is here, you better find it before it's under a runway."

"And if Huon is here, we should find him before he gets into trouble." Saff smiled, but it didn't quite reach his eyes. Good, the more he questioned the situation, the better.

"Maybe I should blow up some of that machinery," Myrta said. "If either are here, they won't fail to notice that."

"The cameras they probably have installed around them wouldn't fail to notice it either," Jude remarked. He had clipped a lead to Tiny's collar and led him to a patch of grass to pee.

"By the time anyone can act, we'll be long gone," Myrta said.

"Until they plaster our faces across the news," Jude replied.

I felt Myrta become enraged, but she held it back.

"Very well," she said in a terse tone, "what do you suggest?"

Jude shrugged. "We could just look around. If someone is here, they'll notice a group of people."

"The subtle approach, I like it," Saff said. "Maybe we should spilt up?"

"No," Myrta said immediately. "We stay together, no matter what." She eyed Khat.

"I'll go wherever I want," he said and disappeared under the car.

That wouldn't be a safe place if Myrta decided to destroy it, but at least he was out of her sight.

"Come along then." Myrta started walking toward the equipment. "Saff, tell me if you feel them somewhere more specific than somewhere *over here*."

"You'll be the first to know," he said.

"Of course I will," Myrta purred. "And you'll be well rewarded if we find them. I know you enjoy fellatio."

He gave her a funny look. "Yes, I do. Who doesn't?"

She patted his arm. "Precisely. If we find one of our friends, or the key, my mouth will be all yours."

"I'll be looking hard then."

"*Very* hard," she said.

He looked to be waiting, but she said nothing more.

"Right then. I suppose we could try shouting out for them?" Saff suggested. He cupped his hands around his mouth and called out, "Kale? Huon?"

No shout came back in return. He tried again.

Still nothing.

"I feel as though we're getting closer," he said. "As though something is pulling me in this direction."

Myrta clapped our hands. "Very good. You're such an asset."

He stopped and looked at us. "You know, I've never been called that before. As ass, yes, but never an asset."

"Such a shame you haven't been appreciated until now," Myrta said soothingly.

He smiled. Was he starting to let go of his doubts about her? Maybe Khat's accusation about thinking with his cock was overpowering his common sense.

"I know, right?" he said and shrugged one shoulder. He resumed walking.

Tiny let out a deep growl.

Myrta turned toward the dog. "They say dogs see things others don't," she remarked. "Can you tell what?"

Jude let Tiny guide his steps and walked past us. "I'm not sure."

Tiny stopped and growled again, more deeply this time.

"Whatever it is, he doesn't like it."

"Huon?" Saff called out again. "Kale? It's us, Saff, Summer and Fletcher. And friends. You can come out now, wherever you are."

A figure stepped out from behind a stand of trees.

I mentally gasped.

CHAPTER TEN

*T*avar?

"What are you doing here?" Saff asked.

"Troll!" Myrta growled. "How dare you enter this realm? Vermin!"

"Summer—" Saff reached out a hand but Myrta ignored him.

She raised our hands and sent a bolt of magic toward Tavar.

The troll yanked a knife out of the sheath at her hip and raised it in front of her face.

If I had any control over my breath, I would have held it.

The magic seemed to take an eternity to cross the

space between us. Tavar was going to be incinerated or blasted into a million minute fragments.

The magic hit the blade square on. The impact drove Tavar back a few steps. Her arms trembled, muscles strained. She bared gritted teeth and let out a low cry.

With a grunt, she swung her arms and the magic flew back off the blade like a ball from a racket. The bolt flew back across the space and struck Fletcher in the centre of his chest.

Fletcher convulsed. His eyes flew open wide. His arms stretched out, fingers spread apart, but curled as if to grab hold of something. Anything.

He convulsed again, starting at his hands and working up his arms, shoulders, upper body—until every part of him shook.

No! I screamed, even though no one but Myrta could hear it. I screamed again and again, until she clapped her hands over her ears.

That won't help you! This is all your— I stopped mid-sentence and stared.

A mist rose from Fletcher's body. At first, it looked like little more than steam rising from a boiling pot. A heartbeat later, it was a roiling cloud.

It coalesced, slowly at first, then in a rush it became a face, an ethereal body, a mouth open in a silent scream. Transparent wings rose behind the figure, gossamer smoke and misty lace.

"What the fuck is that?" Saff exclaimed.

"Cyrir..." Myrta sounded genuinely emotional, regretful.

"Myrta..." The figure spoke once, then dissipated, blown away on the light morning breeze. In a matter of moments, he was gone.

Fletcher fell to his knees. He wove in place for a moment, then toppled sideways to the ground.

Fletcher!

"Fletcher!" Saff ran and crouched beside him. He put two fingers to his throat.

Everything and everyone froze for a dozen heart-beats, maybe more.

Saff turned around slowly and looked at Myrta. "He's alive. Khat was right, wasn't he? What are you?"

"She's a nympha," Tavar replied. "She's infested Summer's body. Her *mate*," she snarled the word, "is dead. Fletcher should be fine."

"How do we get her out of Summer?" Saff asked.

Myrta bared her teeth. "You don't. She's almost gone from this body." She waved a hand toward Fletcher. "Cyrir was insignificant."

Liar.

"Our mission remains unchanged. We get the keys."

"Um, you might need this." I had forgotten about Jude, but he'd removed his shirt and handed it to Tavar.

She gave him a funny look, but shrugged into it anyway. "I had forgotten humans are prudes."

"Trolls don't belong in this realm," Myrta growled.

Tavar arched an eyebrow. "The portal sucked me in and sent me here. I would suggest not only do I belong here, but whatever powers are controlling us want me to help further." She put her knife away.

"Lucky she didn't kill you then," Saff said.

Fletcher groaned and started to rouse.

Saff gave Myrta a last side-eye, then turned his attention back to him. "Hey, Fletch. Buddy? Come on big guy, you're alive."

"I can feel that," Fletcher moaned. He rubbed his head and winced. "It hurts like a motherfucker." He cracked his eyes open and squinted.

"Is that just you?" Saff asked.

"Um, I think so." Fletcher wriggled his fingers. "I did that myself. Thank the gods. How—" He sat up slowly. "Tavar."

She inclined her head. "Fletcher."

"Thank you. Your knife…" He frowned.

"It has certain properties," she replied. "And some unexpected side effects."

"Oh really?" Saff asked. "You didn't know he was inhabited by a nympha, did you?"

"I had no idea," she admitted. "I was trying to send the magic back to its source." She looked firmly toward Myrta. "If you try to use magic to harm me again, I won't miss this time."

Myrta scowled. "You have no idea who you're dealing with—"

"It doesn't matter. I possess the means to kill you and I will use it," Tavar's voice was ice.

"Can you do it now?" Saff asked. "Get her out of Summer!"

"I can't," she said regretfully. "You don't have the right kind of magic and a mere blade would kill them both."

I don't mind! I shouted. *Get rid of her and you'll be safe.*

"Well, we don't want Summer dead," Fletcher said.

I wanted to cry. Finding the keys and saving the Fae realm was more important than one Fae. They needed to get rid of Myrta before she killed one of them, or got her greedy bitch hands on the keys. If I died, then I died.

"I suppose we can guess where your other two friends are," Jude said softly.

"Yes, darling," Saff managed a smile and helped Fletcher to his feet.

Jude snorted softly. "Yes—Darling. Harbour. Are we taking her?" He jerked a thumb toward Myrta.

Good point, I said, *leave me here. I'm a liability. Well, Myrta is.*

"We can't leave Summer, even if she's infested," Saff replied. "She's the anchor. Until we can get Myrta out of her, we need her. Kale will find a way."

Myrta laughed, a nasty, bitter sound. "By the time we find the others, your precious Summer will be gone. You need me to get the keys, without or without her."

"You know, I really don't like you," Saff remarked.

"Neither do I," Fletcher said. "You're not nice. Even Cyrir hated you. He kept telling me about you."

I saw a flicker in his eyes. I couldn't put my finger on what, even if I had control of my fingers. He knew something.

"Lies," Myrta declared. "Summer cannot hear my thoughts. You couldn't have heard his." She didn't sound so sure.

He didn't respond.

"I guess we should go then," Jude said. He looked uncomfortable without his shirt, but when we got back to his car, he opened the back and pulled out a fresh one with a smiling skull on the front.

"Shame," Saff muttered. He looked away and gestured toward the back seat. "Myrta, you can sit in the back with Tavar and I."

"I am not sitting next to a troll," she growled.

"I prefer not to not sit beside an evil nympha who inhabits the body of my friend," Tavar remarked. "However, there's more at stake than who sits beside whom."

Saff looked from one to the other. "I'll sit in the middle."

Khat slunk out from under the car and eyed us all. "One of them is gone." He sniffed at Fletcher. "Nice work." He flicked his tail at Tavar. "Troll," he greeted.

"Mimicat," she replied.

"Your doing?" he asked.

"Indeed," she replied.

"The other one remains," he stated.

"For now." Tavar nodded and patted the knife at her hip.

Myrta snorted. "When I am a god, you will worship at my feet."

Khat tilted his head. "How about…no," he replied.

She regarded him down her nose. "I didn't mean you. I will eradicate mimicats, along with trolls and other such vermin."

"That's hypocritical, coming from someone who took over the body of a Fae," Khat remarked. "That sounds like vermin behaviour to me."

"I think parasite is the word you're after," Fletcher said as he slipped into the passenger seat.

"Ah yes," Khat agreed, "so it is. I stand corrected." He jumped into the back of the car and Tiny followed, curling himself into a ball as everyone else climbed in.

So, I said after having been silent for a while. *Fletcher was able to hear Cyrir. That's interesting. Have you tried talking back to me? Oh wait, let me guess. That's beneath you.*

She lifted our chin.

You're all alone in the world, with people who hate you, I told her. *The moment they realise they can find the keys without me, they'll kill you.*

"They need me," she said out loud.

Saff turned and gave her a funny look. After a moment, understanding dawned on his face.

"Summer is talking to you, isn't she? Tell her I love her."

Tell him I love him too, I said.

"I am not your messenger," she snarled.

"I wasn't—" Saff stopped. "You weren't replying to me, were you? She said she loves me back. Didn't she?" He looked thrilled.

"I don't think now is the time," Tavar told him.

He glanced toward her. "Of course it is. It means she's still in there." He turned back. "We'll get you out of there, whatever it takes, all right?"

I trust you, I said, even though I knew he couldn't hear. Maybe it would show in my eyes. *Yes, they're still my eyes, you parasitic bitch.*

"She told you to give up and let her go," Myrta said, looking smug.

"No she didn't," Saff replied. "The Summer we know will fight until the end. She'll fight until she is dead, or you are."

"You're overestimating her resilience," Myrta said.

He's really not, I told her. *I will not give up, not for a moment.* I was ready to do that only a few minutes before, but the expression on Saff's face renewed my resolve. I would get free or find a way to take her with me.

"She just contradicted you, didn't she?" Saff grinned. "That's my girl. Hang on, we'll find the others and get you out of there."

"If I didn't need you to find the keys, I would kill you now," Myrta said.

"Lucky for me you do then," Saff said. "Lucky for you, we need you too. Well, Summer. I'll just have to think of you as—I don't know, a flea—in the meantime."

"An intestinal worm might be more appropriate," Fletcher said over his shoulder.

"He's right," Jude remarked. "If Summer was a dog, I would give her a deworming tablet."

If it would get rid of Myrta, I would take it," I said.

"When I'm a god—" Myrta started.

"Save it," Saff said. He waved his hand in dismissal. "Soon you'd be nothing but a bad memory."

"You seem very certain for a Fae who knows nothing about the world," she remarked. "Any world."

"I know plenty," he replied. He looked as though he was about to add more, but stopped and wrinkled his nose. He made a horrified face. "Oh gods!"

What is it? I asked frantically. *Saff?*

He turned away and put a hand over his face. "Oh gods," he said again, "really?"

Saff? What's going on?

"I'm so sorry," Jude said from the front, further confusing me. "He gets like this when he eats canned dog food.

Gets like what?

Saff sounded as though he was choking.

My anxiety went into overdrive, sure he was about to die.

Myrta gagged and pinned our nostrils between our fingers. "What is that smell?" she asked.

"Tiny farted," Saff said from behind his hand. He laughed at the expression on Myrta's face.

I mentally sagged. Was that all? If their faces were anything to go by, the odour must be horrendous. For once, I didn't mind not having control over my senses.

"He'll be doing that for a while now," Jude said. He wound down the window beside him, but those in the back of the car remained shut.

It's not too late to get out of my head, I said happily. *I'd hate for you to asphyxiate.*

Myrta grumbled, pressed our body back into the seat and shook her head. "I'm adding dogs to the list of things I'll eradicate."

If I was able to move my head, I would have thrown it back and laughed. Instead, I sat back to enjoy her discomfort. I hoped Tiny would fart all the way to our next destination. Seeing her like this was worth every bit of flatulence.

Good boy.

CHAPTER ELEVEN

"Saff, can you shrink the car?" Jude asked. He glanced toward Myrta, his eyes laced with suspicion and confusion. He knew I was still in there, but he was right not to trust her with his vehicle. Gods, he barely knew me as it was, much less this monster who wore my body.

"I can," Saff replied.

We rounded a corner into a narrow alley, just out of sight of the street. Everyone bundled out, but they all kept a distance from Myrta. That was as it should be, but I felt isolated enough, being stuck in here.

Saff shrunk the car and Jude stuffed it back into his pocket.

"They could be anywhere around here," Fletcher

said. He looked tired, but no worse for wear, considering his ordeal.

I couldn't help the stab of envy that he was free and I wasn't. If the bolt of magic had hit me, instead of him... Judging by what he said, Cyrir might have let him go if Myrta was gone already. We might both be free of them by now.

I sighed mentally. The point was moot. The magic had hit him and it was done with now. I couldn't let despair overtake me. That, however, was easier said than done. Every moment that passed, I felt more and more of myself slip away into nothing. Soon, I would cease to exist. They would find the keys without me. Myrta might win, or she might not, I'd never know.

"Let's head toward the water," Jude suggested. "If they flew to land, they might have stayed nearby."

"That sounds like them," Saff agreed. "Huon probably found a bar and is having beer and waiting for us."

I smiled to myself. That *did* sound like Huon. Kale, on the other hand, would be looking for a way to contact us.

As if correctly interpreting my thoughts, Myrta asked, "Saff, can you sense them?"

He frowned at her and looked very much as

though he didn't want to respond. Eventually, he nodded.

"I sense something like I felt when we found Tavar," he said slowly. He turned in a circle and shrugged. "All I get is *somewhere* around here."

"Can you try to be more specific?" she snapped. "Surely you must be able to control your magic enough to do that?"

"Nope," he replied easily. "That's the best I can do. Take it or go away. Maybe without Summer's body you can look around more quickly." He gave her a dirty look.

She scowled and muttered something about useless Fae under her breath.

"Very well, which way is the water?" she asked.

Fletcher gave her a quick glance, then headed off in a northerly direction, toward the busy streets. Everyone hurried to follow, but in the press of pedestrians who made their way through the city, the going was slow.

"Are you sure there's a harbour this way?" Myrta asked after a while.

No one bothered to respond.

We continued down a sloping street and onto a footbridge. That led to a set of winding stairs which ended at the side of an expanse of water.

"The harbour," Jude stated.

"Yes darling, it is," Saff said, with only a hint of his usual humour.

Jude gave him a half smile in response. "That's the International Convention Centre." He pointed to a building with a glass facade. People moved around inside it.

"Restaurants and bars are the other direction, down there." He waved to the right.

"Let's start there," Saff said. "If we don't find them, we can at least get a drink."

A grin flicked across Fletcher's face, but was gone almost as soon as it was there.

I hated seeing them like this. Our easy banter got ridiculous at times, but it helped the bond between us to grow stronger, and eased the tension of the whole, 'trying to save the world' thing. Now, everyone was tense, drawn tighter than the string on a musical instrument.

If I could go back in time, I'd stab Myrtle in the eye with a fork. Why a fork, I don't know. There was something satisfying about the idea of using cutlery to prevent her from inhabiting my body.

"Wait," Khat said. He sat down and held up a paw.

"There are probably dozens of stray cats—" Fletcher started.

"Shhh," Khat urged. "There's something else here. Something…"

"Worse than a nympha?" Tavar asked dryly. She gave Myrta a side eye and a smirk.

"Not worse, not better," Khat replied, "just different. It's—"

"Out of place," Saff said. "I feel it too. It's like…" He rubbed his chin.

"Like a dog fart in the back of the car?" Jude suggested.

Saff smiled, but it died as quickly as Fletcher's had. "I can't put my finger on it."

Without another word, he stepped off in the direction of the restaurants.

Myrta stiffened. She was as perplexed as I was, I felt it. "If this is some kind of trick—"

We followed the others, but no one looked back at us. We skirted around the water, close enough to see shapes flitting about under the surface. Probably not Seafae. I wished they were. They'd probably help us. I remembered how one had dragged Saff under the water and almost drowned him. They hadn't, of course, they just wanted to deliver a message. In this case though, they might participate in a drowning, if it meant saving the realms from Myrta.

"It's around here somewhere," Khat said.

Saff nodded his agreement. "It and them," he said softly.

"Yes," Khat said, "I feel that too. But does it have them?"

"I don't know, do they have it?" Saff asked.

"No offence, but you two aren't making much sense," Fletcher said.

"Do we ever?" Saff gave him a guileless look.

"Well…" Fletcher shrugged. "I suppose not, but you're making less now. What is this *it*?"

"Please don't say it's a clown," Jude said with a grimace. "I hate clowns."

"Same here," Fletcher said, "but I don't think they mean that kind of *it*."

"Thank fuck for that," Jude said. He hung on to Tiny's leash as the dog growled and raised his hackles.

Well shit, I said.

"For once, I agree," Myrta muttered.

There in front of us were Huon and Kale.

Any sense of relief I might have felt was squashed at the sound of a scream. It didn't come from either of them, but from one of the dozens of screamspinners which hung from the buildings and the enormous web they'd constructed between them.

Webs which Huon and Kale hung in, suspended ten or more metres above the ground.

Shit. Shit, shit, shit.

"What the hells, how did they get here?" Saff asked. "They don't usually exist in the human realm."

"Ugh, I hate screamspinners." Khat shuddered.

"Wh... what are those?" Jude stammered.

"Big fucking spiders," Saff replied. "They must have come through the portal."

Let me guess. They didn't exist the last time you were in the Fae realm?

"No, or we would have eradicated those too."

Is, 'eradicated,' your favourite word?

She didn't respond.

A screamspinner screamed again. It sounded like any human or Fae, but a lot more bloodcurdling.

A scattering of humans who stood around and watched in horror, let out a ripple of fear. None, I noticed, lowered their phones to stop filming.

Huon waved a hand, apparently the only part of him not stuck to the web.

Saff waved back. "Huon, it's good to see you."

"You too," Huon called back. "Any chance you can get us down from here?"

"I have suggested everyone clear the area." Kale nodded toward the gathered humans.

"It's not every day you see man-eating spiders in Darling Harbour," one of them called out.

Man-eating? That's sexist, isn't it? Screamspinners eat females too. With any luck, they'll eat me.

"Not before I blast them to oblivion," Myrta muttered.

So much for keeping a low profile.

A news crew arrived and started to set up beside us.

"Have they eaten anyone yet?" the cameraman asked. He seemed almost excited at the prospect.

I mentally clapped a hand to my forehead.

"Not yet," a human called out. "So far they've only caught those two."

They must have caught Huon and Kale as they were tossed out of the portal.

"Did anyone bring bug spray?" Fletcher asked, only loud enough for Jude, Saff and I to hear.

"Would that work on them?" Jude asked.

Fletcher shrugged. "It would be worth a try."

Tell them they need to shrink them, I said. *They'll be easier to deal with that way.*

Myrta growled in the back of our throat. "Summer suggested we shrink them," she said reluctantly.

"What do we do with all the people watching?"

Jude asked.

"I have an idea," Fletcher said. "I'll be right back." Before anyone could respond, he ran off in the direction we'd come.

"I guess we wait then." Saff crossed his hands over his chest and tapped his foot.

"That's annoying," Myrta snapped.

"Good," Saff replied. "I don't mind annoying you. You're annoying me by inhabiting the body of the woman I love."

"Remind me again why we need you," she said darkly.

"For my good looks," he retorted.

She snorted. "You're delusional."

He smiled. "I'm all right with that. It's better than being a genocidal maniac."

"The realms will be reborn—"

"Yeah, yeah." He waved a hand. "Save it. I've heard it all. We'll find a way to stop you."

Fletcher came trotting back, several spray cans in his arms. He handed one to Jude and gave another to Saff, but ignored Myrta altogether.

"I don't know if this will work on the scream-spinners, but if we spray while Saff shrinks them, people will assume they're working."

Brilliant. I wished he could hear me say that.

"Brilliant," Saff enthused.

Fletcher blushed. "Thanks. I bought lighters too. If spray and shrinking doesn't work, we can turn these spray cans into flamethrowers and set the spiders on fire."

Jude perked up. "That sounds like fun."

"Yeah, it kinda does," Fletcher agreed. "I got the idea from my cousin Flynn. He claims to have fought off monsters using spray cans."

Saff glanced at him and grinned. "You'll have to tell us the rest of that story some day."

"I'd be happy to." Fletcher handed out lighters and tucked his in a back pocket.

"Saff, are you ready?"

"Absolutely," Saff agreed. "I'll try to avoid shrinking Huon and Kale too, in case they get free and get swatted or stepped on."

Fletcher nodded. "Good plan. All right, let's do this."

Myrta stayed back, so I got a good view of the guys approaching the screamspinners.

The spiders eyed them warily and waved legs at them as if to scare them off. One, slightly larger than the rest, screamed at them.

"We're not scared of you," Fletcher called out. He managed to keep any tremors out of his voice.

He brought up the spray can and aimed it at the closest screamspinner. The spray hit the creature in the centre of its body. It hissed. When it seemed as though nothing was going to happen, it withered down and disappeared from sight.

The humans gathered around cheered. If they knew what to look for, they would have noticed Fletcher's head move as his gaze followed something along the ground. He stomped and ground his shoe against the concrete beneath him. He lifted his foot and nodded, satisfied.

One down, a couple of dozen to go.

"That was fair dinkum awesome!" someone in the crowd yelled.

Fair dinkum?

Fletcher and Jude sprayed several more.

Saff moved his hands in front of his groin, obviously trying to avoid drawing attention to himself.

Every now and again the guys would stomp at the ground, but I suspected several spiders scurried away and disappeared.

The remaining screamspinners became more and more agitated. Most fled to the top of the web, but the largest climbed until it reached the roof of the nearest building. It scurried along for a few metres, then stopped.

Look out! I tried to shout, but Myrta remained silent.

The screamspinner crouched, then leapt off the side of the building and dropped toward the guys.

CHAPTER TWELVE

*W*hat are you doing? I railed. *We need them!*

Myrta flicked one of our hands and the screamspinner shrank to half its size before it landed on Jude's shoulder.

"We don't need him," she said. She laughed softly when he cried out in surprise.

He jumped, but the spider clung to him. He batted frantically at his shoulder with the spray can, but got himself as often as he hit the spider.

"Jude!" Saff turned and raised his hands. Before he could shrink the screamspinner, it leapt from Jude and lunged toward my body.

"Blast it!" Tavar urged.

Myrta, who was about to do just that, stopped

and ducked sideways instead. The creature landed on the ground and hissed.

"You think me a fool, troll?" Myrta growled.

"Not at all," Tavar replied. She stepped away from the half-sized spider and drew her knife.

"I'll shrink it more," Saff said.

"No," Tavar said, her tone urgent. "Shrink the others. Get the king and Kale free."

Saff looked confused, but did as she asked. "Fletcher, Jude, I need your help."

Myrta didn't know where to look, which was fortunate because she kept looking from the guys to the screamspinner mere metres from our feet, and back again.

Several screamspinners scurried away over the rooftops and were gone, but Saff shrank the rest.

"They're going that way," a human shouted. Most of them ran off in the pursuit of the giant creatures.

What could go wrong? I thought dryly. No doubt the human authorities would take care of it from here. Hopefully before they reproduced and overran the city. The spiders, not the authorities. Although...

Saff looked around and picked up a sign from outside what looked like a restaurant.

It read, 'Please wait to be seated.' He raised it over his shoulder and swung it toward the web. It stuck to several strands but tore a hole in the base of the web.

He pulled it back and struck again. And again.

After a few blows, the web began to collapse.

Huon and Kale dropped several metres in one go. Both let out a cry of surprise and flailed slightly.

"Try to keep still," Khat called out. "You'll stick more otherwise."

Everyone's attention must have been on the web, since no one remarked on the presence of a talking cat.

Huon and Kale froze, even when they both dropped again. They now hung only two metres off the ground. Near enough to jump down if they could get free.

"Hold on a bit longer," Saff called. He hit the web again and the remaining strands broke into shreds.

Huon and Kale tumbled to the ground and lay in the tangle web which still stuck to their clothes and hair.

The humans who remained to watch, let out a cheer and hurried to help the Fae to their feet. They pulled strands away and some tucked it into pockets as souvenirs.

Thank the gods, I said, partly because I was

relieved and partly because I knew it would irritate Myrta.

I felt her freeze.

What?

Our eyes travelled down. The screamspinner had taken advantage of her distraction and had leapt onto our legs. It crawled upward slowly.

"Summer!" Huon called out.

I heard Fletcher say something like, "It's not Summer." He grabbed Huon's arm to keep him from running toward us.

"Get it off me," Myrta hissed.

"I think not," Tavar replied.

Screamspinners bite, I said cheerfully. *Apparently they've decided to let you die.*

"You'll die too," she said between gritted teeth.

I'm all right with that. I sat back and resigned myself to my life ending. At least I wouldn't feel the pain of the spider's venom as it entered my veins.

"If we die, the Fae realm is doomed," Myrta said. "They need me."

If you've seen anything, it's how resourceful my guys are. They will find a way without you, and me. I honestly believed that. As nice as it might be to be needed and wanted, they would get by and find the keys.

"You could blast it away," Tavar suggested.

"Not without damaging this body," Myrta snarled.

"I could cut it off," Tavar held up her knife and gave a nasty smile. "I might miss though."

Myrta's gaze flicked to Saff. "Shrink it," she insisted.

Saff looked from her to Tavar, then shook his head. "Sorry, I can't do that. Why don't you?"

Myrta raised shaking hands.

It's only shrinking, I taunted. *No big deal. Just don't miss and shrink my body instead of the screamspinner. It'll be on us faster than you can blink.*

The creature climbed higher.

Myrta made a desperate sound in the back of our throat.

Time stood still for a long moment.

The screamspinner reared on its fifth back leg, fangs extended from inside what passed for its mouth. It hissed.

I felt a jerk and a wrench, then found myself looking down at the spider from the front of my own mind.

With a flick of my wrist, I shrank it and stomped on it with my boot.

"Where did she go?" I asked.

"Summer?" Tavar asked.

I gave her a quick smile. "It's me, where's Myrta?"

"I saw something leave your body," Saff replied. "It was gone before I saw what direction it was headed. I...I think she's probably inhabiting someone else." He looked regretful. "She didn't go into any of us though. Thank the gods for that. She was starting to get on my nerves."

I took his hand, pulled him to me and kissed him hard on the mouth. "We'll find her," I assured him. "And we'll—what do the humans say? We'll end her."

Jude nodded.

At least I had their lingo right. Some of it anyway. Someone would need to explain later what *fair dinkum* meant.

"She won't be far," Fletcher said. He looked tired, but relieved. "She'll still want the keys."

"Yes. She won't give up on those," I agreed. That reminded me. I found Kale still peeling pieces of web from himself, but otherwise he seemed unharmed.

"Do you still have the first key?" I asked.

He patted his pocket and nodded. "I do, and it's pulling toward the second one."

I sagged in relief.

Huon grabbed me around the waist. "It seems like you have quite the story to tell."

"I could say the same to you two," I told him. "I don't think bringing screamspinners into the human realm was part of the plan."

Huon grinned. "What can I say? We arrived in style."

"That's one word for it." Saff clapped Huon on the back. "Although since you were about to become lunch, I'm not sure it's something I'd be happy about."

"It just *looked* like we were lunch," Huon said. "In actual fact, this was all part of our plan to save Summer from whatever the hell was in her. Right Kale?"

Kale regarded him, his expression deadpan. "If you say so," he replied. "It does seem as though the creatures helped her to get free."

"Can you answer some questions?" A man from the news crew stuck a microphone into Kale's face. "What was it like being stuck in a web, surrounded by giant spiders?"

"There's still enough web left if you want to find out," Huon replied cheerfully. "We can help you up there."

"Um, no thanks." The reporter backed up a step. "Can I just get a quote for the news? It'll really help my career."

"When you put it that way..." Huon clapped hands to his cheeks and widened his eyes. He looked right into the camera.

"It was the most terrifying ordeal of my life. I owe heartfelt thanks to the incredible, quick-thinking people who saved our asses. Can I say asses on TV?"

"Yes, yes that's fine." The reporter waved for him to continue.

"Where was I? Oh, yes. If not for them saving us, we would have been gobbled up, and those horrible creatures would have moved on to eat the rest of the city!"

I put my hands over my mouth to keep from laughing out loud.

"Thank you," the reporter signalled for the cameraman to stop filming. "You'll be the headline on tonight's news. Come on, Bob, let's get this footage edited." He hurried away, the cameraman in his wake.

"Should we really let them put that on TV, for all the world to see?" Saff asked.

"It'll be all over the Internet by now," Fletcher said. "Don't worry, people will forget us pretty quickly. All they'll think about is spiders, especially with a few still roaming around Sydney."

"I'm not sure I should be happy about that," I said dryly. "Maybe Myrta went into one."

Saff gave a choking laugh. "That would be ironic. She'd be terrified of herself."

"Who would have thought an ancient, evil being would be an arachnophobe?" Fletcher said. He looked amused, but gave me a long look. Only we would understand how it felt to be under the control of the nympha.

"It sounds like we have a lot to discuss," Kale said.

"Should we look for the key first?" Jude asked.

Huon gave him a funny look.

"This is Jude." I gave a brief explanation of how we had met and how he'd helped us.

"He's gay," Saff interjected.

Huon nodded. "Okay, great. Sorry, but can we eat before we look for the next key? We haven't eaten since we got here."

"Good idea," I agreed. "One question though. Why didn't you use magic to get yourselves out of the web?"

Kale rubbed the back of his neck. "When we came out here, we were over the ocean. The scream-spinners spun webs around us before we could so much as open our wings. Apparently something in their webs neutralises magic."

"And they can walk on water," Huon added.

Fletcher shuddered. "Just what we need."

"On the upside," I said, "I'm back and ready to blast them all into chunks of spider flesh." As long as Myrta didn't find her way back in.

"Hurray for dead spiders," Jude said.

I nodded my agreement, then snagged a piece of web from what was left. There wouldn't be much for long. Humans had wandered back and started to collect their own pieces.

I shoved mine into my pocket and saw the others were doing the same thing. Evidently, they'd come to the same conclusion I had.

"I don't think we can stay here," Fletcher said. "People are staring. More news crews will be along too. Although, they might just use social media footage instead of leaving their offices."

Jude grunted. "Sounds about right. There are places we can get a meal back the way we came. Waccas and whatnot."

"Waccas?" Huon asked.

"Yeah, they sell hamburgers and stuff. They're a big chain here in Aus."

"Ham…burger?" Huon looked just as confused.

"You've never had a hamburger?" My eyes widened at him.

He shook his head slowly.

I grabbed his hand. "You have to try one. They're amazing. And fries. What do you call them here?"

"Chips," Fletcher supplied.

"Oh yes. Those are *so* good too." I grabbed Saff's hand with my other one and the guys and Tavar fell in around us.

"Chicken nuggets for the mimicat," Khat said.

"You might like their fish burgers," Jude said.

"I'll try both," Khat replied.

"I'll have them all," Huon declared. "I'm starving."

"I hope they serve salad, " Kale said.

"I'm sure they do," I assured him. I turned and looked back. The web was almost gone, but Myrta was out there somewhere. She would come for us, I had no doubt of that.

When she did, we'd be ready.

CHAPTER THIRTEEN

I patted my belly. "I'm so full."

Saff sat beside me on the couch and groaned. "Me too. Can we take that food back with us when we go home?"

I laughed uncomfortably. "When the veil is fixed, you can come back and eat all the fried food as often as you want. Although, you might not want to eat as much as we just did."

Huon flopped down on the other side of him and nodded. "I know I said I was starving, but I think I overdid it."

I sat around so my back was against the side of the couch and my feet were stretched over their laps.

"I suppose we should work it off," I said. I knew

we had to hunt down the key, but it was late already. One more day wouldn't hurt us.

Huon proceeded to tug off my boots and massage my feet. I groaned in pleasure and closed my eyes.

"Working it off sounds good," Saff agreed. He took my hand and massaged my palm and up and down each finger.

"Oh great, they're multiplying," Rick's voice made me snap my eyes open.

"It's nice to see you too," Fletcher said dryly. "Rick, this is Kale, Huon and Saff."

Rick muttered something and stalked toward the kitchen.

"We got food for you," I called over my shoulder. "You're welcome."

I heard the crackle of a paper bag, followed by silence. Apparently, our peace offering was accepted. A, 'thank you,' would have been nice, but if he wasn't being snarky, then I'd take it.

Finally, Rick reappeared with a plate laden with greasy fast food and sat in an armchair. He switched on the TV which sat against the wall and turned to the news.

"Care to explain this?" he said between mouthfuls.

There, in living colour, was the web of screamspinners. Huon and Kale hung in the strands. That was followed by Huon's over the top performance and Fletcher and the others with spray cans.

"What's to explain?" Fletcher shrugged. "Just another day in my life right now." He didn't even sound bothered.

"That's what worries me," Rick said. "You realise none of this is normal, right?"

"Oh, it's pretty normal where we come from," Saff said. "As a matter of fact, I think the human realm is a lot stranger than ours."

"I think it's pretty even," I remarked. "It's all about what you're used to."

"That's true," Saff conceded.

"I don't want to get used to giant spiders roaming around Sydney." Rick scowled at us. "What's next, a plague of talking cats?"

"You wouldn't be that lucky," Khat remarked. He and Tiny had curled up together on a beanbag which was too small for the large dog. His back legs and tail sprawled across the carpet beside it.

"Thank goodness for small mercies," Rick murmured.

"Who is this?" Tavar appeared, still damp from a shower. Her hair hung wet over her shoulder and she was back to being bare breasted.

Rick jumped out of the chair so quickly his plate fell onto the floor. Tiny lunged toward the food and dislodged Khat, who rolled and landed on the carpet, his back arched.

"What the fuck are you?" Rick demanded. His gaze went from her chest to her face. His mouth hung open.

Tavar smirked. "I'm a troll. What the fuck are you?"

"One of the people who owns this house," he replied, his eyes narrowed. "What else are you going to drag in?" He glanced toward Fletcher.

Fletcher looked at me. "Fae, a troll and a mimicat, I think that's it, right?"

"Unless you count the evil nympha which occupied both of our bodies for a few hours today," I said lightly.

Rick's eyes widened. "A... what?" He flopped back onto the armchair.

Fletcher explained in a few words. "So, one is gone for good as far as we can tell. The other is out there somewhere."

Rick slammed his fist down on the armrest, which might have had more impact if it wasn't heavily padded. "This is what I get for leaving you alone today, isn't it? I knew I should have stayed and kept an eye on you." He rubbed his forehead and rocked back and forth for a moment.

"I'm capable of looking after myself," Fletcher replied, his voice tight.

"Yes, he is," I said. "It was his idea to use the spray cans. If not for him, we might still be there dealing with screamspinners and Myrta."

"Agreed," Kale said. "He was extremely helpful and resourceful."

"He saved our asses," Huon said. "Jude too."

Jude blushed. "I should probably get home and explain what all that was." He waved toward the TV. "I'll try to come back in the morning to help search for the key."

I nodded and gave him a smile. "All right. Thanks for all your help so far. We couldn't have done it without you."

He looked pleased, then turned to rouse Tiny, who was licking burger from the carpet. The dog didn't look pleased to be going, but he rose and trudged after his human.

"Oh good, now I get this all to myself." Khat stretched out on the beanbag and proceeded to snore.

"Well," I said slowly, "I'm tired. I think I might go

to bed." I looked at Saff and Huon through my lashes. "Are you two tired too?"

"No," Saff replied with a grin. "I could stay up for a few hours longer."

"Perfect," I told him.

"Me too," Huon said. A smile played around the corners of his mouth.

"All right then." I swung my legs to the floor and gave Fletcher and Kale a regretful look. Fletcher might be better to stay down here and placate his brother.

And Kale—well, I still wasn't sure where we stood. We hadn't had much time for conversation. I would have to make some time, maybe after we found the second key.

Rick didn't look up as we walked past and headed up the stairs. He said something under his breath, but it seemed to be addressed toward himself. With any luck, he wouldn't give his brother any more of a hard time than he already had.

"Fletcher was nice enough to let me use this room." I opened the door. "His is directly opposite. I assume he'll find the others somewhere to sleep."

"Lucky the bed is so big." Saff sat and bounced on the end a couple of times. "There's plenty of room for all of us."

Huon grinned and moved to lie against the pillows.

"You're a bit overdressed." I took off my trousers and kicked them aside.

"He is rather." Saff pulled off his shirt and dropped it on the floor.

"I was almost food for screamspinners," Huon said. "Maybe I deserve some spoiling." He placed his hands behind his head.

"You might be right," I replied. I slipped out of the rest of my clothes and helped Saff with his.

We climbed onto the bed beside Huon. I gave him a cheeky smile before I pressed my mouth to Saff's. My hands slid down to cup his rear, while he caressed my breasts.

I cracked an eye open to look at Huon. "How's this?" I asked between kisses.

"It's a start." He nodded.

"I think we need to give him more," Saff said. He left my mouth and kissed his way down to my breasts. His tongue teased one nipple before he locked his lips around it and began to suck.

I let out a soft moan from the sheer pleasure of his touch, and Huon's eyes on us. Knowing he was watching aroused me so much I thought I might come with a touch.

"And more." Saff worked his way further down. He gripped my hips lightly and turned me around so when he parted my legs, my pussy was in full view of Huon.

"That's so pretty," Huon breathed.

"I'll bet she's tasty too." Saff bent to lick gently at my folds. "Mmm, she is." He licked a little more firmly, then hooked his arms under my legs. Open to him like that, his tongue caressed my clit with even strokes.

"Oh gods," I breathed. My hands curled into fists. I wanted to hold on, to make this last forever, but seeing Huon staring drove me closer and closer to the edge.

Just before I tilted and went over, Saff pulled his face back.

"Time to give Huon a little taste," he said, his voice husky. He sat up and undid Huon's pants. "Summer is right, you're overdressed for this." He pushed Huon's pants down and drew out his erection.

"I don't want to disappoint anyone," Huon said. He moaned as Saff leaned down to run his tongue over the tip of his cock. "Gods, Saff..."

Saff grinned and helped him out of the rest of his clothes. He stroked Huon's length while Huon moved himself to the space between my legs.

Huon flicked his tongue against my clit. Slowly, he slipped a finger inside me, then another.

"So wet and warm," he said, as though he never touched me there before. He leaned in again to tease my clit with his tongue.

From the corner of my eye, I saw Saff move down Huon's body and take his cock into his mouth.

Huon groaned against my folds. His fingers thrust into me, in and out, in and out, keeping rhythm with Saff's sucking.

"Can I come?" I whispered. Could I stop myself?

Huon picked up his face, his mouth glistening. "Yes, you may." He licked me more deliberately now, driving me closer without hesitation or mercy.

In turn, I bucked, riding his tongue to the cliff edge and off.

My back arched as an orgasm washed over me, so intense I bit my lip to keep from screaming to the sky. It carried me away to a place where only pleasure existed amidst the roaring of blood in my ears and around my body.

When I came down, Huon smiled at me and slid his fingers free.

Saff picked up his head and grinned.

I looked from one to the other. "I think we're

neglecting Saff a little." I held up my hand to him and pulled him up and over me.

"We don't want to neglect Saff," Huon agreed. He sat back, but I pulled him over toward me too.

I wound my legs around Saff, until his cock was pressed against my pussy. With my free hand, I guided Huon's cock to my mouth.

"On three?" Saff said jokingly.

I giggled and sucked Huon's tip as Saff pressed his cock into me.

Huon groaned and pushed himself deeper. "Good girl. I love fucking your mouth," he said softly.

I couldn't speak with a mouthful of cock, so I grunted in reply and sucked his length while Saff pounded into me, thrusting harder and faster by the moment.

The groans of both men sang like a harmony in my ears. Feeling both of them inside me drove me fucking wild.

I took Huon right down to the back of my throat. His response, in return, heightened mine. His hips bucked as he thrust.

Saff pounded faster and faster, deeper and deeper until I was sure they would both split me in two.

I wasn't sure who came first, but the other was only a heartbeat behind. Both pounded frantically, while I tightened my mouth and my pussy around them, milking them both for every drop.

Their groans, in almost perfect unison, pushed me back over the edge. I had to pull back from Huon's cock so I could breathe, while the most powerful orgasm I had ever had spun me around in a whirlpool of passion and dragged me down into depths I would happily have drowned in.

When my head finally cleared, I found both guys beside me, matching pants coming from their mouths.

My heart gradually slowed and fatigue took the place of excitement.

"Who said you could come?" Huon whispered teasingly.

I laughed softly. "I did." There was no way I could have held back. Not this time. "You're both incredible."

"You're not bad yourself." Saff sounded sleepy.

I laughed again but that was all I did before sleep claimed me.

CHAPTER FOURTEEN

*S*ome time before dawn, I showered and crept downstairs. The house was still in darkness. Somewhere from outside, an animal made a strange laughing sound.

I startled, let out a squeak and pressed a hand to my chest.

Once my heart slowed again, I stopped to really listen. It was a weird sound, but definitely not a person or a screamspinner. I decided it was harmless.

Hopefully.

"It's a kookaburra." Rick's voice sounded in the gloom.

I jumped again. "A what?" I laughed to cover my

embarrassment at being scared twice in a short amount of time.

"It's a kind of bird." A light clicked on. He stood near the kitchen sink, his face lined, weary. He didn't look as though he'd slept much, if at all.

"I see. They sound interesting," I said politely. I stepped around him and turned the electric kettle on.

His eyes stayed on me the entire time. "I suppose they do." He paused for a moment before he spoke again. "Why are you here?"

"I thought I'd make some tea and toast," I replied.

He snorted. "That's not what I meant. I mean, why here? Why Australia? Why my home?"

I saw the unasked question in his eyes. *Why my brother?*

I exhaled softly. "To be honest, I don't know. Fletcher made his way to the Fae realm without me. It was sheer luck I found him at all. Otherwise he might still be stuck down there, in the dark." Near the room where the dark magic artefacts were locked behind an ordinary-looking door.

"Seems like one hell of a coincidence." He leaned against the kitchen bench and crossed his arms over his chest.

"It would be if it was one," I agreed. "I don't think

any of this is. Someone, long ago, knew dark magic would draw lesser magic to it. They left a failsafe if it did. We just happened to set it off."

"Or it was set off and it was you who answered," he suggested. "Maybe Fletcher's presence is still a coincidence."

"Maybe," I agreed. "But not mine, Saff's or Kale's. Tavar's too, if the portal sucked her through. I still think Fletcher has a role to play."

"A human, a Fae and a troll walked into a bar," he muttered.

"Exactly," I replied.

His head jerked and he stared at me. "What?"

"Fae have visited the human realm for generations," I replied. "Some humans know about us, but most don't. Few humans reach the Fae realm but never without a Fae. Trolls working with both—it's unheard of. That it's happening now speaks a whole library of volumes about how important this all is."

"To you," he said. "Not to the human realm."

The kettle clicked off and I poured tea into a cup, over a teabag. While it steeped, I turned back to Rick.

"I think the two realms are inextricably connected. If the Fae realm dies, the taint will cross over to this realm. No offence, but the human realm is polluted already. Add the taint and life as you all know it could be gone in a few blinks."

His eyes narrowed. "You really believe that, don't you? You're not trying to screw me around so I'll let Fletcher work with you."

I held back an eye roll, although it was almost painful. "He can make up his own mind," I said coolly. "But yes, I do believe it. If we don't succeed, Fae, trolls, humans, even mimicats, will all die out."

He nodded slowly. "You said Tavar got dragged into this world."

"That's right," I said carefully. "Trolls are abundant in the Fae realm. They live and hunt in tribes and keep knowledge the Fae has long forgotten."

"You make them sound civilised," he said dryly.

"I was as surprised as you are," I told him. "They keep to themselves and so do we. I didn't think of them as any better than animals until I met them."

I squeezed the excess water out of my teabag and dropped it into the rubbish bin.

"There's always room to change our minds about people." I gave him a pointed look and curled my fingers around my mug.

"It's not people who concern me," he replied, unflinching. "It's the shit they get involved in. And get me involved in." He grimaced.

I shrugged. "You could help save the world. Isn't that on everyone's to-do list?"

He stared at me for a moment, then barked a short laugh. "You're something all right."

"I try." I fluttered my eyelashes.

"I'm sure," he replied. "So, there was a reason I asked about Tavar and the portal."

I cocked my head. "I can't guarantee nothing else came through, but it should be mostly harmless. Mimicats are irritating, but screamspinners are the worst that—"

He held up a hand to cut off my flow of words. "I can guarantee something else came through. Unless mermaids were already here. Or merchicks. Whatever the word is."

I frowned and shook my head. "I'm not sure I understand what you're asking. Saff saw a Seafae, but…"

He pulled his phone out of his back pocket and turned it on. After a moment he held up a photo of something which looked like a Fae, but with the tail of a fish. She had long, dark hair, which billowed out behind her in the water.

I blinked, but the image was still there. "What the hells?"

Rick sounded as stunned as I was when he said, "I

work at the aquarium. That—she came swimming up alongside me. Scared the shit out of me. At first, I thought it was a joke. Then she showed me her tail, let me touch it. She sounded like you when she talked. Same weird accent."

I ignored the insult and peered closer at the photo. "She certainly looks like what Saff described. You think she got pulled in too?"

"You tell me."

I ran a hand over my hair, tugged the ends, and shook my head. "I can't be sure unless I meet her. Where is she now?"

"I smuggled her into one of the back tanks," he replied. "I didn't know what else to do." For the first time since we'd met, he looked rattled.

"The aquarium," I said slowly, "that's near where the screamspinners were."

"Another non-coincidence," he said dryly.

"Agreed." I sipped my tea. "I was hoping to go looking for the key, but I think we need to see her first." Given the way things happened so far, she too was here for a reason. I smiled slowly. "I guess you were meant to work with us too."

He scowled at that. "I don't like the idea of anything I do being governed by some—higher power. I've read enough Greek mythology to know gods, if there are such things, get a kick out of screwing with humans."

"Oh really? These Greeks know there are several gods?"

"Ancient Greeks," he replied. "They had dozens. My favourite is Zeus. He got all the women."

I shook my head and smiled. "Humans and Fae aren't so different, really."

He smiled, then his expression closed. Any sense I had gotten from him that he was warming to me was gone. He didn't look as hostile as he had, but he didn't look friendly either.

I sighed to myself and went to grab bread to make toast.

"The others should be awake soon," I said. "Then we can go and see this Seafae of yours."

"She's not mine," he said tightly. "I just happened to be in the wrong place at the wrong time."

Even though his renewed antagonism annoyed me, I said, "Another human might have killed her, rather than help her."

He paused, then gave a rough shrug. "I suppose so. Or put her in a tank, on display. Maybe I still should; she'd make me rich."

"Money won't help you if the world ends," I pointed out.

"It would help me for a little while," he said. "I could buy so much booze I could miss the whole apocalypse. And enough women to screw while it happens."

"Well, everyone needs ambitions, I suppose." I pulled my toast out of the toaster and slathered on too much Nutella spread.

"Yes," he replied. "We fucking do. By the way, that offer still stands."

This time I let out an eye roll in all its glory. "Thanks, but I'm satisfied already."

"Another time then." He started to unpack the clean dishes from the dishwasher, but every now and again he would glance at me.

"What?" I asked after a while.

"Nothing," he said.

"Liar," I accused cheerfully.

"Fine." He stood straighter. "I was just wondering what would have happened if I ended up in that place in the Fae realm where you found Fletcher."

"Oh, that's easy." I waved a hand in the air. "I would have left you there."

He threw back his head and laughed. "Now who's the liar? You wouldn't have left anyone behind in a place like that."

I had to concede the point. "I suppose I wouldn't, but I might have let the beetles eat you."

"Now *that* I believe," he said.

"What do you believe?" Fletcher appeared behind me and snaked an arm around my waist.

I turned my face for a kiss on the mouth and nestled into him.

"He thinks I'm mean," I replied with a pout.

Rick snorted and went back to emptying the dishwasher. While he did, I told Fletcher about the Seafae. Rick showed him the photo and he gaped at it.

"Why didn't you say anything yesterday?" Fletcher asked.

"Yesterday was all about giant spiders," Rick replied defensively. "And trolls. I was struggling to get my head around it all. I'm surprised you've managed."

"Was that a compliment?" Fletcher asked, an eyebrow raised.

"Call it whatever you want, I kept the merchick to myself then. Today, I shared."

"Seafae," I corrected.

"Seafae, merchick, whatever. Call her a bloody fish woman if you want to. Whatever she is, she'll be discovered if she's there too long. For the sake of whatever sanity I have left, you need to get her out of my tank." He put down a plate so hard on the bench it split in two. "Fuck. That was my favourite," he cursed.

"You have a favourite plate?" I asked, bemused.

"Not anymore," he said sourly.

I held back a laugh while Fletcher patted his brother's arm in conciliation.

"There are other plates out there, buddy, better plates. Plates which cannot be—"

"Yeah, yeah." Rick shrugged him off. "Make fun. I dare you. I know which coffee cup is your favourite."

"The one with the rainbow swirls?" I'd seen Fletcher use it once or twice since I'd been here.

"No," Rick replied. "It says, 'adulting is overrated,' on the side."

"It is overrated though," Fletcher argued. "I only use that mug on special occasions. Like after we save the world."

"We'll have reason to celebrate," I agreed. If we succeeded. There was still a chance we wouldn't, or Myrta would interfere. Still, I had to assume we would be triumphant. I had to stay positive. If I let too many doubts enter my mind, they would drag me down.

"We'll need all that booze then," Rick said.

"We?" Fletcher looked surprised. "It's we now?"

"As much as I don't want to get involved in any of this," Rick said, "I've been dragged in by you too and your merchick."

"Seafae," I insisted.

"Whatever." Rick looked unconcerned.

"I think I hear the others starting to get up," I said, grateful for a reason to move away from Rick. I had reached my limit of tolerating his prickly behaviour.

"Good, let's hope you don't have any more shocks for us," Rick said before he stomped away.

CHAPTER FIFTEEN

"This can't be good," Saff said.

"Oh?" I asked. "Why is that?"

"I'm pretty sure that's the same Seafae who tried to drown me." He cocked his head at her.

"You were never in any danger." She leaned against the edge of the tank, her arms on the side. Her tail was covered in blue scales in several shades.

No, I corrected myself, it was more than her tail. Her scales went all the way up her chest, to her collarbones. Where she might have breasts, she had small mounds, but no discernible nipples. Maybe they were under her scales, and maybe she simply had none. Either way, she looked more fish than Fae.

"My name is Yina." She drew out the I as though it was two EEs instead.

"Have you come to help, or were you also drawn in by accident?" I asked.

"Oh, I'm very much here deliberately," she replied. "In fact, you're all here because I brought you."

"You couldn't have us all arrive in the same place?" Huon asked. He learned against a wall, his arms crossed over his chest, looking mistrustful.

"You couldn't leave the screamspinners behind?" Khat—shrunk so we could smuggle him in with us—stuck his head out from Fletcher's shirt. He jumped down and eyed her as though she might be good to eat.

"That was an unfortunate accident." She looked totally unconcerned.

"That's one word for it," Huon said dryly. "We could have been a snack."

"But you weren't," Yina replied.

"But we could have been," Huon insisted.

"Why did you bring us here?" Kale said. "Why this country?"

"You don't like Australia?" Her pout was worthy of me.

"You brought us here because it's where I live," Fletcher guessed.

"And close to the second key," Kale added. "But—not close enough."

"It was as close as I could get us," Yina said.

"Us?" Rick echoed. "You didn't mention an us yesterday."

"You weren't receptive yesterday," she said calmly.

"You Fae realmers..." Rick spluttered. He stalked away, but over his shoulder he said, "Hurry up, I shouldn't have even let you all in here. It'll be my job if they find you."

I caught a glimpse of Fletcher's expression. He obviously wanted us all to get along, including Rick.

I shook my head, I couldn't think about that now, I did move closer to Fletcher and slipped my hand into his.

He shot me a grateful look and a faint smile. I returned it with a nod and turned my attention back to the Seafae.

"So, where is the key?" Huon was asking. "Don't say it's at the bottom of the ocean."

Personally, I didn't see a problem with that, if Yina could get it for us and bring it back. Kale, Huon and I almost died to get the first one. If we could avoid unnecessary risk, then I was all for it.

Of course, nothing would be that simple.

That was apparent a moment later when Yina

shook her head. "I found the place, in a manner of speaking."

"I like puzzles, but can you stop speaking in them, please?" Fletcher asked.

Yina sighed as though he was being obtuse. "The key is on an island outside the harbour, but I can't reach it. Or see it."

"How do you know it's there?" I demanded. On the scale of things which made sense, versus complete nonsense, this sat around the middle, but my patience was wearing thin.

"How do I know you're there?" she asked.

"Uh, you have eyes?" I suggested.

She huffed. "Because I sense you there. You're judging me."

"To be fair," Saff said, "we're *all* judging you."

Huon snorted. "He's right about that."

"Indeed," Kale said.

"If you didn't need my help, I'd leave you alone to find the key by yourselves." She flicked her hair over her shoulder.

I raised a hand in a conciliatory gesture. "I'm sorry, we don't mean to be difficult, we've been through a lot in the last couple of days. It would be nice if something was simple and easy."

"If it was either of those things, others would

have found it by now." Her voice got higher as she spoke. "They might have released dark magic into the realms and created any number of twisted and horrible—"

Huon cut her off. "We get it. We can deal with hard, right, Sum?"

"I can deal with hard," I replied, "but I prefer my *puzzles* less difficult. So where is this island?"

"I'll have to take you there," she said.

"I can't swim," Khat said.

"So… you can stay behind with Tiny," I suggested. The dog was outside with Jude, who opted to stay there rather than risk the dog being stolen. "I'm sure he'd happily share the beanbag again."

Khat made a rude noise and his tail flicked. "I think I'll keep looking for my mate."

"And by mate, do you mean any cat in heat?" Saff asked with a grin.

"As if you can talk about animals in heat," Khat retorted.

"I regret nothing," Saff said.

"Neither do I, except we're wasting time here," I said. "We need to get to this island and get the key." I was growing tired of this quest. I wanted to get home and release lesser magic. I wanted to see the trees recover and the flowers bloom. And then I wanted to spend a week in bed fucking my guys. Was that too much to ask?

"I need help to get back out of this tank," Yina said. She held up her arms like a child demanding to be picked up and held.

I snorted and stepped back.

Kale moved forward and hooked his arms under hers. She wound hers around his neck and smiled at him. If he noticed, he showed no sign of it. He simply swung her against his body and settled her in place.

"People are going to notice your tail," Huon pointed out. "I think we've given the humans enough to look at already."

Tavar grimaced at that. She wore one of Fletcher's hoodies, which hung to the middle of her thighs. The hood was drawn up over her face, so only her mouth and eyes were visible. Rick said she looked like a criminal, but he hadn't elaborated. That was probably just as well, since she looked ready to put a knife in his gut for his trouble.

Fletcher murmured his agreement and slipped off the hoodie he wore. "Better we don't let them see your wings either," he said. He lay the fabric over her tail and tucked it into the sides.

Yina wriggled slightly. "That tickles."

"Just tickles?" Huon asked. He flashed me a cheeky smile. He knew better than most how sensitive my wings were.

"Yes," Yina replied, "what else would it be?" She gave him a funny look, but all he did in response was to chuckle.

"Do you always think with your cock?" Khat asked scathingly.

"Do you?" Huon retorted.

"Touché." Kale hefted Yina up a little higher and led the way toward the exit.

"I think we've established we all think with our cocks," Saff said. "Except Summer and Tavar, who don't have them." He eyed Tavar. "At least, I assume."

She gave him a dry look but didn't answer.

The room Rick had led us to was at the rear of the aquarium, in a section for staff and whatever sea creatures they housed there. Either none had occupied the tank, or Yina ate them. Having taken a few bites of a fish burger the night before, I was in no position to judge.

The way out to the section open to the public was down a corridor lined with various rooms and a general air of salt water and sea creatures.

At the end of the corridor was a locked door. On the wall to the side was a panel with numbered buttons in it. Some of the numbers looked more worn than others.

"It's a keypad," Fletcher said. "We need a code to get out." He glanced around and frowned. "We need Rick for—"

"Who are you and what are you doing here?" a voice demanded.

"Shit," I said under my breath. I turned slowly and plastered a smile on my face. "Hi, we got lost. Is this the way out?"

A tall woman with spiky hair and a scowl on her face regarded us. Was everyone who worked here grumpy?

"I said who are you?" she demanded.

Fletcher stepped forward. "My name is Fletcher. My brother works here—"

"No one is allowed to bring family back here," she growled. "What is his name?" She pulled a phone out of her pocket and pressed it to her ear.

"Um."

I had a feeling Rick was about to get in big trouble.

"You could just let us go," Yina said. "We're not causing trouble."

The woman's brow creased deeply. "What's wrong with you?"

"She's a paraplegic," Fletcher said quickly.

"Why do you have a cat?" the woman demanded. "None of this is allowed here." She clicked her tongue.

"Really, you should let us go." Yina's voice took on a strange quality.

I shuddered. What the hells? Was she using some kind of magic?

I didn't know of any magic that could control the minds of others, aside from inhabiting their bodies.

I almost laughed out loud at myself at the thought. If the last few days taught me anything, it was how little I really knew, especially about magic. Gods, I wouldn't have suspected a thousand year-old magic could last, much less control my actions and those of the people around me. This was small in comparison.

"What's the pin code?" Fletcher asked gingerly. Whatever Yina was doing, he felt it too and was leery of breaking her concentration, or that of the hapless staff member.

The woman didn't even blink. "One, three, one three," she said in a monotone. Something flicked across her eyes, a hint of fear and confusion.

I immediately felt terrible. The memory of Myrta in my head, using me to speak and act was all too raw. To see it happen in front of me made my stomach twist.

"Press the code in," I said, my voice tight. "We need to get out of here. Now." I grabbed up Khat and tucked him under my shirt.

"If you scratch me, I will hurt you," I told him.

He hissed but pressed himself closer to me.

Fletcher pushed the buttons. The door clicked and popped ajar. He pushed it the rest of the way and stepped through.

I gestured for Huon to follow him, and Saff after that. That left me standing beside Kale, while Yina's attention was still on the woman.

"I can make her forget," Yina said. "Move me closer, I need to touch her."

"This better work," I muttered.

"If it doesn't, then we can kill her. Then she definitely won't recall anything."

I shivered at the coldness in the Seafae's tone.

"I'm sure that won't be necessary," Kale said firmly.

Yina touched the woman's forehead with the tips of her long fingers. "Turn her around," she ordered.

I took hold of the woman's arm and moved her gently until she faced the other way. Her feet shuffled, but her expression remained blank.

"Go back to work," Yina told her. "We were never here."

The woman walked away, without so much as a glance over her shoulder.

"There." Yina lowered her arm. "Simple. I'm surprised you didn't do it yourself." She arched an eyebrow at me.

"I didn't know I could," I told her. I wasn't sure I even wanted to try.

"Hmmm," she huffed. "Maybe you can't. Shame."

"Right." That might be for the best. I followed her and Kale through the doorway. Before I closed the door behind me, I looked back but saw no sign of the woman.

I sighed softly. The sooner we found the key and got back home, the safer everyone in this realm would be.

CHAPTER SIXTEEN

"*T*he mimicat should come," Yina said once we'd stepped into the public section of the aquarium.

The ceiling and walls were made of glass. It held back the gods knew how many tons of blue water and dozens of fish. A flat one with a long tail passed right over my head and made me shiver.

"It's a stingray," Fletcher said.

"That name doesn't fill me with confidence." I turned to Yina. "Why do you think Khat needs to come?"

Khat peeked up at me. His ears flicked back and forth, tickling my skin.

"Mimicats can sense danger," Yina replied. "Better than any Fae, or even a troll."

"I'm sensing some now," he said. "I sense following her will be dangerous and I should stay behind."

"It sounds as though we need you and your wisdom," I told him. "Who better to keep us out of trouble?"

"Oh sure, appeal to my ego," he said sourly. "Fine, I'll come, but if I die, I'll come back from the hells to haunt you."

"Noted," I said. I turned to Fletcher. "So why isn't this glass falling in on us?"

"Be careful what you wish for," Khat said darkly.

"Are you doing the wishing?" Saff asked. "All those fish, raining down on us…"

"If I have to die, there are worse ways to go than drowning in fish," Khat agreed.

"There are better ways too," Huon pointed out. He grinned at me.

I replied with an eye roll.

"Look, Daddy, a mermaid!" A little girl stood a few metres away and pointed toward Yina. "I told you they're real!"

I froze.

The girl's father stepped beside her and put a hand on her shoulder. "I think it's just a dress up,

Caitlin," he said. "But it's a very well made one." He smiled and nodded to Yina.

"Daddy!" Caitlin exclaimed. "It's called cosplay. No one calls it dress ups anymore!"

He held up a hand in surrender. "Sorry." He smirked at me. "I guess it's an age thing. It was dress ups last week."

While I returned his smile, Caitlin put her hands on her hips.

"Daddy, you're embarrassing me!" She spoke so loudly her voice echoed. A few people stopped to look and shake their heads before they shuffled on.

"Caitlin, shhh," Daddy urged. "People are staring."

"Your dad is right, you know," I told her. "Hey look, a stingray!" I pointed toward one which swam toward us.

Her eyes wide, Caitlin turned to watch it glide past.

"We should go," I said out of the side of my mouth.

"Can I touch your costume?" Caitlin had turned back and now pointed at Yina's tail, where it peeked out from under the hoodie.

"Caitlin." Her father reached for her hand. She ducked away from him and stepped forward a few steps.

"*Pleeeeeaaasssse!*"she begged. "It's so pretty!"

"Of course you can, child," Yina said with a gracious smile. Now she had dried a little, her hair looked to be a shade of green.

Caitlin darted forward, put a hand on Yina's scales and darted back. Her eyes huge, she said, "It feels like a real fish! How did you do that?"

"Just a bit of magic," Yina told her.

"Magic is real?" Caitlin asked in awe.

"Naturally," Yina said. "You just need to know where to look for it."

"Wow," Caitlin breathed.

"Um, thank you." Her father took her hand and led her away with a tug. The girl looked over her shoulder every few steps, her mouth agape.

"Lucky she didn't hear the talking cat," Saff remarked.

"Indeed," Kale replied. He led the way down the glass tunnel toward the door leading back out of the aquarium.

"Or see Fae wings," Huon added.

"Or stare at my scars," Fletcher said.

He sounded so wistful, I curled my arm around his and walked tucked up against his side. "Where is your brother? I thought he was in this with us."

"I thought so too." He glanced over his shoulder.

"I'm sorry about him, I know he can be difficult, but he means well."

"I'm sure he does," I replied, if only because I hated the idea of the two being at odds with each other. "He did tell us about Yina after all."

"Did he?" Fletcher asked.

I glanced at him in surprise.

"Maybe he told us and maybe she coerced him to do it," he explained.

My mouth formed an O. "It could have just been him, trying to help," I said tentatively.

"I suppose I shouldn't assume otherwise." He sighed. "But after seeing what she did... Do you think you could do that too?"

"I don't know. Maybe I'm doing it now and I don't realise." I frowned. "Maybe it's magic causing you all to be nice to me?"

He leaned into me and chuckled. "It might be, but it's not mind control. It's just you and your own special kind of spell."

Khat made a disgusted sound and popped the tip of his nose out from my shirt. "Do you want me to puke on you?"

"Not particularly," I replied.

"Then stop being so nauseating, both of you." His head disappeared again.

"Sorry, not sorry," I said cheerfully.

"I have claws," he muttered.

"I'm sure we can arrange to feed you to the sharks." Fletcher grinned.

Before Khat could reply, Rick appeared at the end of the tunnel, a scowl on his face. He gestured for us to hurry.

I glanced at Fletcher in confusion and quickened my steps.

"Where have you been?" Fletcher asked him.

Rick drew himself up. "Getting us a boat."

I blinked. "We were going to fly—"

"A boat is good," Khat declared.

"It might indeed be easier to sail than fly or swim," Kale said. "We can all travel together. Assuming this boat fits us all?" He raised an eyebrow at Rick in question.

"It should." Rick looked uncertain and gave a half shrug. "We'll find out. It's this way." Without another word, he turned on his heel and headed out toward the harbour.

I walked quickly to keep up with him before he rounded a corner toward a boat moored alongside a wide walkway. Judging by the way the craft was tied to a light-post, I guessed this wasn't the normal place to park one.

"We shouldn't be stopped here, so get on board."
Rick barked. He grabbed the side and vaulted into
the boat. "There are lifejackets under each chair. Put
them on."

"What about—" I started to say.

"We're here," Jude called out. He and Tiny trotted
toward us, both puffing lightly. "We saw you come
out of the aquarium. Well, Tiny did." He stopped and
patted the dog.

"Uh, should we take the dog with us?" Huon eyed
the creature.

"We can't leave him behind," I said. "He's one of us
now."

Jude grinned. "He loves boats." Evidently Tiny
agreed. The moment he got close, he leapt inside.
Jude was forced to let his leash go before he was
pulled face first into the harbour.

Tiny, apparently not bothered by the way he
caused the boat to rock under his sudden weight,
scrambled across the small deck to the front and
stood, tongue lolling out, as if to say, "Let's go!"

Jude chuckled and climbed inside, then turned
and offered me his hand.

If this was anywhere else and any other time, I
might have refused. I would have spread my wings
and flown onboard. But this was here and now and

we'd already drawn too much attention to ourselves. So, I took his hand, stepped over the side and into the craft.

It rocked under my feet, making my stomach uneasy.

"It'll be easier if you sit down." Rick waved toward the seats in the centre of the boat. His tone was actually nice. So much so I looked at him in surprise, but he faced the other way and took Yina into his arms when Kale passed her over.

The Seafae looked as comfortable being on water as she did in it. Rick sat her down on the seat in front of me and she settled in as though it was Fletcher's beanbag.

Saff flopped down on one side of me and Huon sat on the other.

"I'm not sure about this boat thing," Saff said. He looked toward the side, but shuddered and sat back. "How will it stay afloat with all of us on it?"

"Magic?" I replied lightly.

"Physics," Fletcher said as he sat behind us. "We don't weigh enough to sink it. There's enough seats for at least twenty people. There's eight of us and Tiny. He counts as two of us. And there's Khat, but he's small, even when he's not shrunk. Even if we were too heavy, some of us could shrink down smaller."

I nodded. "That makes sense." To Saff I said, "See, we'll be fine."

He regarded me for a long moment, then said, "Tell me you're not as scared as I am."

I licked my lips. The boat rocked as Rick stepped across to the controls.

"All right, I'm a bit scared, but not worried. We have magic and wings if anything goes wrong."

"That's the spirit." Huon patted my thigh, then left his hand there.

"Right," Fletcher agreed. "You might get a bit wet, but you won't go down deep."

I looked at him over my shoulder. "I feel as though that's worth a good score, but under the circumstances I can't give you one. The idea of going deep underwater is terrifying."

Saff murmured his agreement.

"Fair enough," Fletcher replied. "I'll take a score later, if you care to give me one."

"Oh, you might score later," I agreed.

Fletcher grinned. "That's definitely a ten."

I shook my head and laughed. "I try." I fluffed the bottom of my hair and smiled sweetly. That faded when the boat started to move and I had to grab the seat in front of me.

"Think of it as a car on water," Fletcher said. "In fact, this is probably safer than being on the road."

"Especially the way some people drive," Jude said with a nod.

"Right," Fletcher agreed. "Luckily for us, Rick drives a boat better than he drives a car."

"I heard that," Rick said over his shoulder. "Lucky the aquarium let me use this at all."

"Do they know we're using it?" Saff asked.

Rick turned back to look at us. "Well…"

I shook my head. "All the more reason to get the key and get back here. We don't want you to get into trouble on our account."

"We don't?" Saff asked teasingly. "He might like our kind of trouble." He gave Rick a wink.

Rick flushed and turned back around.

"See, no one can resist my charms." Saff puffed his chest out.

"Of course they can't." I patted his knee, then quickly returned my hand to the seat in front of me. "You're adorable."

"Not as adorable as me," Huon said. "I might even execute anyone who disagrees." He fought back a smile.

"Hey, you wouldn't execute me," Saff protested.

"We might not execute you, but we might throw you overboard," Huon said. His face was pale, even a little green. He was obviously trying to lighten the mood to take his mind off the action of the boat.

"You forget, I have a Seafae to save me," Saff said lightly. "Right, Yina?"

She arched her eyebrows at him. "You are necessary to finding the key."

"That's me, *necessary*," he said proudly.

"Then, when we have the keys, you might not be so important," she added.

He sagged, deflated by that. "We could say the same about you, I suppose," he said weakly.

"Indeed, you could," she agreed. "In the meantime, we should focus on the task at hand. Think about the key and that will guide us to it."

"Why do I get the impression it won't be that simple?" I asked.

She turned her face away and didn't respond.

CHAPTER SEVENTEEN

"Hey!" The passengers on board a larger boat called out and waved vigorously.

"Nice dog!" a young man shouted, his hands cupped around his mouth.

Jude and Saff waved back.

I kept my grip firmly where it was, but managed a smile. Whether or not they saw it, I didn't know. I don't suppose it mattered too much anyway. They seemed happy just seeing a dog drool all over the deck of a small boat. Why wouldn't they be, they didn't have to clean it up.

Under other circumstances, I might have enjoyed travelling across the harbour. The breeze on my face kept my stomach from twisting and turning too much. From the water, more of the city was visible, houses, skyscrapers, the bridge and the opera house with its sails. I preferred nature, but it had a beauty of its own.

Today, I couldn't appreciate it. I sat with my eyes half closed and waited for some sign of the key to reach out to me.

For some reason, possibly just pure arrogance, I wanted it to be me who found it, or at least led us to it.

Let's be real, it didn't matter who it was, as long as we found it.

"Why can't you lead us right to it?" I asked Yina, my tone more accusing than I intended. "You seem to have a better idea of where it is than we do."

"I can guide, but no more than that," Yina replied coolly. Which was no real answer at all, if you ask me.

"In other words, you don't know where it is either," Huon said. "It's calling to you like it's calling to Kale, but that's it."

She turned to look at him down her nose. "It's on an island and I have no legs," she replied. "You're correct, I don't know the specifics, but I suspect it will take more than one to retrieve it, like the first key."

"How did you—" Huon frowned.

"I was able to extract the knowledge from Saff's mind," she said.

"Are you Myrta by any chance?" Saff asked.

Yina's face turned red and she actually hissed at Saff. "The Seafae are ancient, but we are not evil. We have spent generations hiding from the nympha and their like. If you had any idea—"

He held up his hands in surrender. "All right, all right, I'm sorry. I just figured I should ask."

I took my hand off the seat long enough to pat his arm. "You were right to ask. Myrta could be anywhere right now." Including on this boat. Even Tiny wasn't above suspicion. Khat would have told us if he knew she was around. At least now he'd be listened to if he spoke up. Later, I would growl at the guys for ignoring him while she inhabited my body. Could they really not tell the real me from the one with an evil parasite inside?

I shook my head lightly. "Are we getting closer? Can anyone tell?"

Kale frowned. "I think so. Or so the first key says."

"But?" I prompted.

"There is something between us and the key," he said slowly.

"Water?" Saff said brightly.

Huon turned his head slowly and smirked at Saff.

"Apart from water," Kale said, a faint smile on the sides of his mouth. "And I am not referring to air either," he added as Saff opened his mouth.

"Someone had to lighten the mood," Saff said cheerfully.

"More jokes like that and we'll lighten the boat." Huon mimed grabbing Saff and tossing him over the side.

Saff made a rude gesture at Huon.

"I'm pretty sure doing that means instant execution." Huon rubbed his chin as if he had a beard and was lost in contemplation. "Wouldn't you agree, Summer?"

I cocked my head at Huon for a moment, my expression serious. Then I made a rude gesture at him as well.

While Huon pretended to be offended, I grinned. "Saff was right, we needed to lighten the mood. Now we have, can we focus on the key?"

I turned my attention back to Kale. "Can you tell what's around the key? A cave maybe? An army of souls?"

"Possibly either," he replied. "Possibly both. Maybe neither."

"Well that clears it up," Saff said sarcastically.

"I'm sorry I can't be more clear," Kale said. "All I know is we're getting closer."

We had left the harbour and were now travelling on open ocean. The water was rougher, the waves bigger. The small boat would crest, then plunge, crest, then plunge.

To keep from being sick, I focused, searched for an island with my eyes and my other senses. All I saw was ocean. All I felt was wind and the sting of salt water. I was about to suggest we leave the boat behind and fly when Kale let out a shout.

"There!" He pointed straight ahead.

I blinked. Squinted. Blinked again.

"I don't see anything," I said after a few moments.

"Neither do I," Huon said.

"Me either," Fletcher remarked.

Jude looked as blank as the rest of us.

Rick looked over his shoulder to ask," Are you sure?"

"I'm certain," Kale said with a nod.

"He is correct," Yina replied. "There is something there. I suspect he feels it stronger than I." For some reason, she looked annoyed at this.

I bit my lip and kept my eyes on the spot of water maybe a kilometre ahead.

"Shouldn't waves crash against land?" Saff asked.

"If there's something there, it would act like a beach. Right?"

"Not if magic is involved," I said uncertainly. "But if there's a beach and we can't see it, how will we get to it?"

"Without destroying the boat," Rick added. "It'll be my job if there's a scratch on this thing."

"Perhaps Yina can swim the rest of the way and pull us in close," I suggested.

Yina hesitated, then nodded. "That would seem to be the best course of action, yes." She gave me a funny look, but accepted Kale's help to the side of the boat.

Muscles straining in a way which made me stare, he lifted her and lowered her into the water.

She bobbed on a wave and wrinkled her nose. "Earth water has a way of feeling dirty."

"Sorry about the pollution," Fletcher said with a sigh. "Some of us are trying to work on fixing that."

She gave a grunt and took hold of the rope Rick tossed her.

He turned off the engine and leaned against the side of the boat. He looked ready to leap into the water with her, if only to prevent any damage to the craft. Instead, he watched with narrowed eyes.

At first, the boat seemed to resist her attempt to

pull it forward. Gradually, the rope went taut and we started to move again.

Yina swam with one arm. She kicked her tail hard, and pushing her forward over the waves, the vessel tugged slowly behind her.

After maybe ten minutes, she stopped and looked back over her shoulder. "I'm in the shallows. I can either drag the boat, or you can—"

She cut her words short when Rick vaulted over the side.

"Rick…" Fletcher stood, hand out, but Rick was gone before his brother could take a step.

"Come on then," Rick's voice sounded from beside the boat.

I let go of the seat and slowly, gingerly, stepped to peer over the side. "What the fuck?"

Rick stood in the churning ocean, but the water only came up to his thighs. "Like Yina said, it's shallow here." He sounded certain, but he looked down toward the ocean and shook his head. "Unless this is just a strange fucking hallucination."

"It's certainly strange," I agreed. The water was white. Anything below the surface was invisible beneath it, including anything which lurked there and wasn't a Seafae.

Huon regarded the whitecaps for a while, then

climbed over the railing and dropped into the water. He landed with a plop, surprise on his handsome features.

I wouldn't admit it, especially to him, but he looked like a king, even in waist deep ocean. A leader. Something good might come out of this quest after all.

"What do you know, they're right." He shrugged and offered me his hand. "Come on, Summer, it's perfectly safe."

"It doesn't look safe," I replied. The way the waves pounded around him, it looked as though he might be sucked under at any moment. In spite of his assurance, I knew he was ready to unfurl his wings and fly if he needed to. Mine twitched. I wanted to take to the air instead.

He glanced toward his feet. "It doesn't feel like it looks, I promise."

"Am I going to get sucked under again?" Saff called out to Yina.

"Not unless it's necessary." She seemed unapologetic.

"Um…" He stepped back from the railing. "Define necessary. I mean, last time…"

"I was forced to do that to assess your intentions," Yina stated. "As I said, we've been hiding for millennia from those who would use dark magic. Had you been one of them, you would have remained under the water."

"Is that a nice way of saying drowned to death?" I asked flatly.

"Yes it is," she replied. "I'm satisfied your intentions are—perhaps not pure, but not evil either."

"Thanks," Saff said, "I think." He scratched his head for a moment and hesitated before he climbed over the side and into the water. He landed up to his thighs, then sank in further. In less than a heartbeat, the water reached his chest.

"Oh gods, you said it wasn't deep!" His eyes were wide.

The water reached his chin. His arms flailed.

"Saff!" I cried out in alarm. My heart raced and rose toward my throat.

Before I could throw myself in after him, he popped back up and grinned.

"Just kidding, it really is shallow." He brushed dripping hair off his face and said, "You should see your expression."

"Let me guess. Does it look like I think Yina should drag you under after all?" In spite of my relief, I planted my hands on my hips and glared. He scared the shit out of me. I wasn't going to let him forget this.

"That's exactly how it looks. Come on in, the water is nice." He patted in front of him.

Fletcher stood beside me, shaking with silent laughter. "I'm sorry, but that was kinda funny."

"Only if he wants to be kinda dead," I replied, but a smile escaped. "I guess it's our turn."

I took a breath but let it out in a rush when Tiny jumped over the side before Jude could stop him. The enormous dog landed beside Saff with a huge splash that drenched the rest of him.

I burst out laughing. "Now *that* was funny!"

Even Tavar, who had pushed her hood off her face now we were away from the crowds, looked amused.

Saff wiped water out of his eyes and spat some out of his mouth. "Thanks, mutt. We make a great team."

Tiny wagged his tail and swam a few metres before he was able to stand. With the ocean raging, he looked like he was walking on water. Luckily the people on the boats we'd passed couldn't see him now. They might make some kind of deity out of him.

"Follow that dog," Fletcher said and gestured toward him.

"Don't forget I'm here," Khat said from inside my shirt. "Mimicats hate getting wet."

"We already decided there are no points for wet pussy jokes, didn't we?" Fletcher asked.

"Yes we did," I agreed. "Those are far too easy, especially with him around."

"And they're not funny," Khat said in my voice.

I stifled a laugh. "That depends on the context." And the pussy.

"Shame." Fletcher shook his head. "All right, do you want to go first, or do you want me to help you get wet?"

I gave him an admiring look. "I think that's an eight and a half."

He pumped the air with his fist. "Almost a nine."

"Keep working on it." I patted his arm, then climbed the railing.

"Get a room," Khat muttered.

I ignored him. "Here goes nothing." I held Khat in place with one hand and jumped into the roiling waves.

CHAPTER EIGHTEEN

Water squelched in my boots.

I followed Tiny, who seemed to be the only one who knew where to go. He happily trotted ahead, then stopped to roll. When he rose again, he was covered in sand.

"There's definitely an island here," Saff said.

His words were redundant, since I already stepped out of the ocean and sunk into sand I couldn't see. Whatever made this island look like the middle of the sea, it was certainly stubborn at giving up its secrets.

"Be careful," Kale warned. "There might be a—"

"Ouch!" Saff rubbed his nose.

"Magic barrier," Kale finished.

"No shit," Saff muttered. "Maybe warn a guy before he walks into it."

"Maybe don't walk around a place under a magic spell," I said. "You could have fallen into a bottomless pit."

"It wouldn't be bottomless then, would it?" He grinned. "Mine would be in there."

"It would once you and your bum fell out the other side," Fletcher pointed out.

I snorted.

"How could I do that if it has no end?" Saff asked.

"I'm sorry, I'm a librarian, not the world's expert on bottomless pits," Fletcher replied.

"I assumed those things were one and the same." Saff looked disappointed.

"It does seem as though they would be, doesn't it?" Fletcher rubbed his chin. "I'll be sure to bone up on bottoms when I get home." He glanced at me.

"Eight and three quarters," I told him.

"A very cheeky score," Saff said.

I groaned. "That only gets a five."

Huon cleared his throat. "Meanwhile, we have a magic barrier here. Kale, I assume the key is behind this?"

"It feels as though it is, yes." He looked back

toward Yina, who remained in the shallows and looked annoyed she couldn't get closer.

"I can feel nothing behind the barrier," she said.

"We need to bring it down." Tavar looked ready to stab it with her knife.

I remembered how she countered magic with it to free Fletcher and wondered what else it might do. Perhaps a magic barrier was right up its alley.

Before I could respond, Huon spoke.

"Do we?" he asked. "What if the island isn't really here? Maybe it's just the barrier we feel under our feet."

"I feel sand." Saff kicked his foot and sent some flying.

"The sea would still wash sand up onto a fake island," Fletcher said. "At least some of this is real."

Rick approached the place where Saff had struck his nose and raised his hands. He pressed his palms against something. "There's something as weird as shit here," he remarked. "It tingles."

Fletcher raised a hand. "Maybe you should—"

Something flashed and Rick was thrown back. He landed with a grunt and a whoosh of air leaving his lungs.

Fletcher hurried to him and flopped down on his knees beside his brother. "Rick?"

Rick groaned and slowly sat up. "Fuckingshit-damcockfuck," he muttered. "Son of a bitch. I don't think that thing wants to let us in."

"Your swearing ability is amazing." Saff gave Rick an admiring look.

"Thanks." Rick rose and dusted himself off.

"We need to find out how far this thing goes," Huon said.

"Or I could blast it," I suggested.

"How are you going to do that?" Huon asked. "You don't know what you're dealing with."

"I have an idea," I said. "Fletcher, did you bring those spray cans?"

He blinked at me and then grinned. He pulled a spray can out of the pack he carried on his back and tossed it and a lighter to me. He then pulled out one of his own, gave me a savage smile, and pressed the nozzle. A floral scented mist sprayed out toward the barrier. He raised the lighter and set the mist on fire.

Flame hit the barrier and blossomed out to either side and upward. Several metres above us, it disappeared. It petered out at the sides before the barrier ended.

"I'm going to try something," I declared. I slipped off the jacket I wore to cover my wings and unfurled them. It felt good to spread them and let the breeze caress the span.

"Wait!" Khat leapt out of the front of my shirt and made himself back to his usual size. "I am not flying with you, especially if fire is involved!" His tail waved in aggravation.

"Suit yourself." I flew a few metres in the air to the place where the flames disappeared. I raised the spray can and repeated what Fletcher did.

I almost jumped and dropped the can when the mist ignited, but hung on and flew a little higher.

There, at the same point as before the flames surged over the top of the barrier. The flash of triumph I felt was short lived.

I released the nozzle and dropped back down to the sand. "I was hoping to get in over the top, but the barrier has a roof." I handed the can and lighter back to Fletcher.

"I suspected as much," Huon said.

"Indeed. Climbing or flying in would be too convenient," Kale said.

"That's one way to put it," Saff said. "What now? Does Summer blast it? Does Tavar use her knife?"

"Maybe you can summon an army of butterflies to pick up the barrier and move it?" I said, only half joking.

Huon clicked his fingers. "If you could get them to cover it, we'd know if it ends."

"Or the butterflies will be incinerated, like I almost was," Rick pointed out. "I need to find a tree to tie the boat to." He started to walk toward the south, his arms outstretched in front of him.

"I'll go with you," Jude said. He whistled to Tiny, who galloped to him and promptly stopped to pee on something invisible.

"Tiny might find you a tree," Saff said.

"At least he would be good for something," Rick said over his shoulder.

"Hey, he's good for lots of things." The sound of their voices tapered off as they wandered off down the beach.

"I'm cautious of trying to blast the barrier." Huon drew my attention back to the task at hand. "If it threw Rick back, it might do the same to any magic we toss at it. I would hate to have Summer blow apart."

"I would also hate that," I agreed.

"There are definitely better ways of being blown," Saff agreed.

For once, I ignored his innuendo. "Tavar, what can your knife do?"

"It absorbs and rebounds magic," she replied. "In a

manner of speaking." She drew it and stepped forward.

"Wait." Huon put up a hand. "What if it absorbs all the magic in the barrier? Is there a chance it might be too much for it? And you?"

She shrugged. "What's one less troll, your *highness?*" She gave him a sarcastic smile and jabbed her blade at the barrier.

For a long moment, nothing happened.

And then… Still nothing.

Tavar lowered her hand and sagged.

"Well, that was anticlimactic." Saff sounded disappointed.

"It was rather," I agreed.

Tavar, apparently not ready to admit defeat, turned to me. "If you blast the barrier with magic, I'll use my blade to deflect the magic if it bounces back to you."

"Well, of course," I muttered. "What could possibly go wrong?"

"No," Huon said firmly. "I'm not going to allow Summer to risk herself like that."

"Allow?" I echoed. "It's not like you have a say—"

"The hells I don't," he snapped. "I'm still your king, and I love you." He flushed while those words hung in the air.

Saff raised his eyebrows and smiled. For once, he said nothing. That was probably just as well. We could have this conversation later.

If there was a later.

Huon swallowed audibly. "We need you for this journey." He turned pleading eyes to me. "*Please* don't do this. We'll find another way." He looked to Kale as though silently pleading with him to have a suggestion, a solution which didn't need me to take this risk.

Kale sighed and shook his head slowly. He gave Huon an apologetic look, but that was all he could offer.

"Someone else then?" Huon said. He sounded desperate now. "I could try. Or Saff."

Saff blinked at him, but he shrugged and nodded. "I would give it a go, but no one blows things up like Summer does. It's kind of her thing."

"Yes, it is," I agreed. "Even if I wasn't, there is no one else to try this. Kale is the foretold, Saff has some connection to all of this. You, as you just reminded us all, are the king. I'm an insignificant Fae who just happens to be able to blow things up. Maybe this is what I'm here for." I shrugged.

"You are *not* insignificant," Fletcher said softly.

"To any of us." He took my hand and squeezed it. "Aren't you the anchor?"

"I was, but that was when we had to find the last key. The gods only know if that means anything now." I squeezed his hand back, then released it. "I'm doing this, so you should all step back." I sucked in a breath and nodded to Tavar. "Let's do this."

"Summer, *please*." Huon begged.

I couldn't bring myself to look at him. If nothing else, I was worried I might change my mind. Then where would we be? Stuck on this beach, arguing about what to do next? We could argue for days and get nowhere.

I raised my hands.

"Wait!" Huon shouted.

I stopped and frowned at him. "What?"

He put his arms around me and kissed my mouth, deep and long. When he finally drew back, he whispered, "Don't you die on me. We have too much left to do."

"I wasn't planning on it," I told him. "I love you too. Now, would you step back before you get blown up too?"

He smiled and hurried out of my way.

"A bit further back." I waved them all another

couple of metres away. "One more step each. No, two more. All right, good."

I raised my hands again, then paused in case another of the guys had something to say.

When none did, I summoned all the magic I could, and aimed it straight in front of me.

A bolt of magic shot from my fingers and struck the barrier. As it did when Rick touched it for too long, it let off sparks. At first a few, then a burst of them.

I squinted against the glare as the sparks grew into a glow. A pillar of smoke poured off the barrier, then the magic gathered in a huge ball and hurtled back toward me.

Tavar leapt in front of me and raised her knife. The magic hit the blade hard enough to make her grunt. She forced it away and fell to her knees. The magic ricocheted off and flew back toward the barrier.

Weaker this time, it still struck with force.

Once again, the barrier smoked and the magic was flung back.

"Shit!" Huon shouted. "Look out!" He flung himself to the side and pulled Saff with him.

I let out a squeak and threw myself to the sand

beside Fletcher. It felt harder than it looked. I winced and screwed my eyes shut.

The magic flew right over the top of my head. It ruffled my hair as it passed. I might have smelled singeing. Maybe a slight smell of burning.

A giant splash tore through the air, followed by a loud explosion. I covered my ears with my arms and hunkered down smaller.

The explosion kicked up a wall of water and sand. It rained on me like a coarse shower. What felt like hours couldn't have been more than several seconds.

Then everything went deathly still.

CHAPTER NINETEEN

I picked up my head and opened my eyes. At first, everything was fuzzy. Light danced in front of my vision, glare from the sparks. I rubbed my eyes.

The roiling ocean was gone, pushed back to the end of a long, wide beach. A gouge marred the sand just above the waterline, as deep as I was tall.

A wave rolled in and the sand started to collapse back into place. At high tide, all signs of the damage caused by magic would be gone.

"Yina?" I pulled myself to my feet and staggered down toward the water. "Yina!"

For a long while there was no response but the gentle lap of waves on the sand.

"Oh gods," I muttered. If my magic killed her...

An arm poked up out of the surf and waved back and forth. The rest of her popped into view a moment later.

"You didn't think I'd stick around with magic flying about, did you?" she called out. She sounded a lot more amused than I felt.

"I guess not," I said under my breath.

"That was lucky," Huon said dryly. He stood with his hands on his hips. He looked somewhere between furious and relieved.

"It wasn't luck," I said lightly. "It was skill."

He looked disbelieving, then burst out laughing. "Oh, yes, of course it was. Silly me. I should have realised you planned to destroy half the beach and almost take out a Seafae."

I batted my eyelashes. "At least I did it with flair."

"That's one word for it." He shook his head. "If you ever do that again, I'll put you over my knee and spank your ass."

I smiled. "Remind me to do that again then." Not. He could spank me when this was all over.

I looked past him to where the others slowly rose to their feet. "Besides, it looks to me like the barrier is gone."

"Along with some of your hair." He touched a section near the front.

I put my hand up to feel, and grimaced. It seemed as though a chunk had been seared away by the wayward—um, perfectly aimed—magic.

"If that's the only damage caused, then I count myself lucky," I replied.

"Your claim to be skilled seems to have slipped slightly," he pointed out.

I shrugged and tried to muster a last sliver of dignity. "It wasn't perfect, but it did the job."

"Not perfect?"

I heard Khat's voice, but it took a few moments to locate him perched in a tree. The one Tiny peed on, unless I missed my guess.

The mimicat jumped out of the tree and slunk toward me.

"We're lucky you didn't kill us all," he said. He gave me a scathing look to match his tone. "I knew I shouldn't have come on this stupid journey. I could have stayed at home in a nice, dark hole and waited for the world to end."

While he spoke, he wandered away, wound through bushes which were previously hidden. I couldn't make out his words, but he kept up a mono-logue the whole time.

"All right then," Saff said slowly and shrugged.

"Kale, can you feel the key now?" I asked.

He nodded slowly. "I sense it clearer, but not its specific location. It could be anywhere on this island."

"It doesn't seem very big." I looked in either direction. Both east and west ended with the beach curling around. It wouldn't take more than an hour or two to walk the length of it. How wide it was, was another question.

"We need to do this quickly," Fletcher said. "An island popping up out of nowhere isn't going to go unnoticed. Before long, we'll have company. And questions to answer."

"He's right," Huon said.

"Are we splitting up again?" Saff asked. "I volunteer to stay away from any water."

Huon snorted softly, but nodded. "Saff, you, Tavar and Fletcher head in the same direction Rick and Jude went. Kale, Summer and I will go the other way."

"What about me?" Khat called out from the bushes.

"I figure you would suit yourself," Huon replied. "That tends to be what you do anyway, so…"

"Right," Khat said. "And don't you forget it." He wound his way back to us and stood beside me. "Well, come on then, what are you waiting for?"

"Nothing at all." Huon looked as though he might add something, but instead he started to walk and left Kale and I to catch up.

"What are we looking for?" I asked, although I know they had no more answers than I did.

"Ruins?" Huon suggested. "A cave?"

"Ugh, not a cave," Khat groaned. "I hate caves."

"Noted," I said. "To be fair, so do I. And tunnels."

"Anyplace dark and corridor-like," Khat added.

"I thought cats like dark spaces?" Huon asked.

"Oh, we do," Khat replied. "It's the danger we object to."

"Ah, I see." Huon parted the leaves of two trees which had grown close together, and stepped through. He held them back for me and I did the same for Kale.

"Watch out for bottomless pits," I told them.

Huon gave me a funny look over his shoulder, but nodded. "That's good advice. The only falling forever I want to do is in love."

Khat made a hacking sound as though he needed to cough up a fur ball. "Please, don't make me bring up my breakfast."

Huon chuckled.

I looked back at Kale. His eyes were narrowed, brow furrowed. He was clearly concentrating on whatever vibes the second key gave off.

"Can you take out the first key and see if that helps?" I asked. "Maybe it'll call out louder?"

He inclined his head, the only indication he heard me. He dug into his pocket and pulled out the first, silvery key. He held it in his open palm. The sun glinted off it. For something ancient, it didn't look very old. I guess magical artefacts held their age better than Fae or humans.

If I hoped a line of magic would light up a sign in front of us which read, "Second key here," I was disappointed. Nothing magical happened, as far as I could tell.

Kale's expression didn't change.

"Nothing?" I guessed.

"Not anything new," he said. "It's just... here somewhere."

"It could be worse," I reasoned. "We could have taken down the barrier and had the key be some-where else altogether."

"Or worse, you could have blown up the key," Huon said over his shoulder.

"I doubt a thousand-year-old key is going to allow itself to be destroyed by a bit of errant—I mean *skilled*—magic," I told him.

"You're assuming it has a choice," he said. He looked back and flashed a smile.

"I know you're trying to goad me, but it won't work," I said. "Kale said the key is here, so it is. Besides, the barrier was here to protect it."

Huon stopped so suddenly I almost ran into the back of him. "What the hells?"

"Was it?" he asked.

"What?" I frowned at him.

"Was the barrier here to protect the key?" His face looked slightly pale.

"And to keep people out," I said slowly. "And to keep this place hidden."

"Or to keep things in?"

His words sent shivers down my spine.

"Like—souls?" We'd released a few to get to the first key. Maybe some were stuck in limbo here too.

"Them," he agreed, "and maybe other things."

"If you're trying to scare me—" I put up a hand to tell him to stop.

He shook his head. "I don't want to scare anyone, but if there's something I've come to expect, it's the unexpected."

I waited.

When nothing jumped out at us, I gestured for him to keep walking. "If you say to expect the unexpected, you'll tempt the gods," I told him. "Do you want something bad to happen?"

"Of course not, but we should be on our guard. The barrier might be one of several obstacles."

"Oh, goody," I said sarcastically. "I know this isn't supposed to be easy, but getting tested over and over is starting to get tiring. Haven't we proven ourselves by now?"

Huon shrugged and led us around a stand of stunted trees.

"It's funny how the sun got in, but nothing else did," I mused.

"What do you mean?" Huon stopped again.

I blinked. "I haven't seen or heard any birds or insects since we arrived. You'd think the magic would have had them screaming in the trees or bushes."

"You're right. Apart from us and the ocean, it's silent here." Huon shuddered.

"Is that normal?" I asked Kale.

"To my knowledge, life exists in many inhospitable places," he replied slowly.

"Like caves," Khat said.

"Indeed," Kale agreed. "Since there is vegetation, air must have existed here all along. There's no reason why creatures wouldn't as well."

"Unless something ate them all," Khat said helpfully.

"Yes, unless that occurred," Kale agreed.

"Can we please hurry up then?" I asked. Goosebumps traveled up my arms; the hairs on the back of my neck rose.

"Good idea." Huon said. He increased the pace, but the bushes became thicker as we went. Some of them bore spiky leaves, or thorns which scratched my skin and snagged my clothes as I worked my way past.

"Ouch!" I caught my hand on particularly nasty one. When I brought my hand up, a bead of blood formed on my finger.

I was about to put it in my mouth and suck it off, when Kale spoke.

"Wait!"

I stopped with my hand halfway to my face. "What?"

"Something changed," he said vaguely.

"Yes, I'm bleeding." The bead turned into a trickle which threatened to run down my finger.

"The key responded," he said. "It's pulling me toward you."

I took a step back. "I'm not a key," I pointed out. Unless the gods were fucking with me and I was an artefact without knowing it. No, that made no sense. The key would have told Kale before now. Right?

"You're not a key," he agreed. "But you might be the key to the key. Or your blood might."

"If you could make sense, that would be great," Khat remarked.

"I agree with him," I said. "What the hells are you talking about?"

"Turn your finger and let your blood drip on the ground," he said. He waved at my hand and nodded.

"Um. As strange shit goes, this is about three quarters of the way up the list, but all right." I tilted my hand and the blood trickled down. It tickled my fingertip. I resisted the urge to wipe my hand clean. I'd never been fond of blood, especially my own.

Where it dripped, a line appeared on the sandy ground. Or to be more specific, a glow of magic, soft and golden. I saw no accompanying sign, with words written on it. Of course not, that would be too helpful.

"So, do we follow that, or run in the opposite direction?" Khat asked. He sniffed at the magic, but kept a safe distance. His back was arched slightly, ready to jump away if necessary.

"He poses a good question," Huon said. "It might point the way, but it might also be a trap."

"It wouldn't be the first trap," Khat said.

"It certainly wouldn't," I agreed. "Probably not the last either." I glanced up at Kale. "What is the key telling you?"

He looked thoughtful and then replied slowly. "It wants us to follow the magic, but I think it's suggesting caution."

"Caution is good," I agreed.

"Yes, we can do cautious," Huon said. "Kale, you should lead if the key is guiding you more specifically now."

Kale gave a short nod and stepped through the underbrush.

CHAPTER TWENTY

"*D*o I have to keep bleeding?" I asked.

Every time the trail of magic started to fade, I squeezed out another drop to illuminate it again.

"We are close," Kale replied.

"You've said that several times already," Khat pointed out. The mimicat sounded as cranky as I felt.

"You really have." I let another drop of blood fall. When it hit the ground, the magic went off at an angle, into the deepest section of bushes yet. Each one was covered in tiny white flowers and thorns the size of my fingernail.

"Please tell me no one will object if I use some magic to *skilfully* clear these bushes," I said.

"I don't know." Huon pinched his nose. "There might be things behind the bushes which magic could destroy."

I narrowed my eyes at him. "Do you really want to walk though all those thorns? Because, personally, I've bled enough. Go ahead, we'll watch." I waved toward the bushes, then crossed my arms over my chest.

He took a step back. "On the other hand, be my guest." He glanced toward Kale. "She can't damage the key, right?"

"It's my understanding the key wants to be found," Kale replied. "I do not think she will harm it in any way." He turned to me. "However, if you damage it, may I remind you it will mean the end of two worlds. Possibly countless others as well."

"I'm not going to do anything like that," I snapped. "What is it with you two? I just want to clear some fucking bushes. Or I could just start with —" I raised my hands toward Huon.

"It's not that I'm not enjoying this exchange," Khat interrupted, "but all three of you are behaving even less rational than normal."

I turned my gaze to him. "What are you—" I blinked at my hands, then forced them back down to my sides. "What the hells? You're right. I feel different too, angry." More than anger, rage. It cooled slightly. If Khat hadn't spoken, I might have...

I shook my head. "Kale, are you sure there's a key here and not something else?"

He looked as if he might snap at me, but he simply frowned. "It's possibly something else, but this key is pulling me toward it."

"Maybe Myrta got here first," Huon replied.

"I wouldn't put it past her to try some kind of fuckery," I said slowly. "But if she had a body, we would have seen her."

"Would we?" Huon shrugged. "We were focused on the beach in front of us, and the barrier."

"Khat, can you sense anything strange here, or evil?" I asked.

"Strange, yes," he replied. "You three. Evil—you have your moments, but I wouldn't say you're that bad."

I rolled my eyes at him. "How about someone or something that isn't us?"

"Not a thing. Perhaps you behaving badly a moment ago was just that, you three getting snappy." He sat down under a bush and licked his front paw.

"No, it's something else, I'm sure of it," I said. "I was ready to blast Huon back to the Fae realm."

"Is that what it was?" Huon said with forced light-ness. "I thought you were going to kill me."

I gave him an apologetic look. "I really want to remove a few of the bushes, so we can get through. We could try to find a way around?"

"Whatever the key is pulling toward, it's amongst those bushes," Kale replied.

"Of course it is," I sighed. "I guess if we pull our sleeves up over our hands..." I proceeded to do just that.

"I think you should just blast the bushes out of the way," Huon said. "What could go wrong?"

"What have I said about saying things like that?" I asked him.

"I'm not sure your instinct to use your magic on him was wrong," Khat said.

"I'm not sure I'd object if you use it on *him*." Huon jerked a thumb toward Khat.

"I wouldn't object if you both stop bickering," I replied. "You also might want to stand back, in case I miss by accident. Or on purpose." I flashed them all a smile.

"I thought you were skilled?" Huon teased.

"I am," I replied. "Hence, I might miss on purpose." Truthfully, my heart raced.

Whatever influenced us a few moments earlier

made me twitchy. I had no reason to think it wouldn't happen again, and I might indeed hurt someone I loved. Or Khat.

Part of me wondered at the wisdom of using magic at all, but I didn't think the bushes and their thorns grew here by accident. They were a simple deterrent if anyone got past the barrier, or if the magic which maintained it had failed. Even animals would avoid digging in the area, if there were animals here to dig.

"All right, here goes. Khat, tell me if I look like I'm going to kill someone."

"Will do." Khat moved a good distance back and crouched on a branch in a large tree. "Try not to have the magic bounce in my direction."

"I make no promises," I said lightly. I sucked in a breath and aimed at the closest bush. A tiny amount of magic and it withered and sank sadly to the ground.

"That was anticlimactic," I remarked.

"In this case, that's a good thing," Huon pointed out.

"I suppose so." I aimed again, with a bit more magic this time. Another two bushes wilted. "I feel bad for doing that," I commented. "We're trying to save the plants in the Fae realm from doing just this."

"I believe humans call it collateral damage," Kale said. "You shouldn't need to harm too many more. The pull is stronger now."

I nodded. The third time I aimed, I felt a strange tug from within the bushes.

"I think there's something—" My initial flush of excitement was washed away by the feeling of whatever drew at my magic. I stopped summoning and tried to pull it back toward myself.

It slipped out of my grasp and took more of my magic with it.

Magic I hadn't summoned.

"Um, guys, I think it's sucking magic through me."

"That sucks," Khat quipped.

"This isn't funny," I said uneasily. "It's taking more and more." Magic moved through me like a blur of light and power. I sensed it building up and up, a glowing ball of stolen force. "I think this was what it wanted."

"I told you not to let her do this," Khat declared.

"The hells you did," Huon snapped.

Their voices sounded distant, as though a cloud surrounded me, muffling them.

"I can't stop it!" I called out desperately. I curled my hands into fists in an attempt to cut off the flow. If anything, it moved more quickly.

Firm hands clamped down on my shoulders and turned me around. "Summer, focus. Let the magic go." Huon looked determined, every bit the king. "Do what I say."

"I can't," I said from behind gritted teeth. "It won't let me. You have to stop it. You have to—"

"I'm not killing you," he said firmly.

"Huon…" I swallowed hard. I was standing in a raging river. I fought the current, but it would sweep me away the moment I became too tired to keep fighting.

Huon grabbed my hands and held them tight.

I squeezed. Even with him holding me, I would be overwhelmed in moments.

"If it saves us all," I whispered, "then you have to."

"No," he said firmly. "I would die before I took your life."

"What about my life?" Khat asked. "I don't want to die."

"Shut up, Khat," I ground out.

"What kind of last words are those?" he complained.

"They're not last words," Huon growled. "Now shut up or I'll put you between her and whatever is sucking the magic through her. It can have yours instead."

"Try a blade," Kale suggested.

My eyes jerked toward him. Of course he would be the sensible one, but it hurt to hear. A tear trickled down my cheek.

"I told you I'm not—" Huon stopped talking. His eyes widened and he drew out his dagger.

I closed my eyes and braced myself for him to strike.

The magic cut off.

Instead of the thunderous torrent, there was silence. Complete and utter silence.

Was this death?

I opened my eyes a crack.

Huon stood with a blade between me and the bushes I'd destroyed.

"Move away slowly," he said carefully. "Far enough it can't feel you and start up again."

I stepped over to Kale. He took my arm and pulled me behind him.

"All right," Kale said slowly. "Lower the knife and we shall see."

Huon nodded. He swallowed visibly and lowered the dagger.

The ground beneath us rumbled.

He hastily raised the knife again, but the ground responded by shaking and groaning.

"Um, I think we should get the hells out of here," I said.

"I agree," Khat replied. He jumped down out of the tree and streaked away through the undergrowth.

"We should get to the beach," Huon said, his voice just below a shout.

Before any of us could take a step, a crack opened in the ground where all the magic went. At first, it was no wider than a hair. A moment later, it was as wide as my hand. And quickly widening.

"What the hells?" I squinted.

Inside the crack, what looked like a boiling river of golden magic bubbled and hissed like lava. Steam rose off it.

"That can't be good," I said.

"Not good at all," Huon agreed. He took my hand and pulled me back.

Half a metre from my foot, another crack opened.

"Maybe not this way," I said.

"Or this," Kale said, as a third crack opened at an angle to the first two.

"That leaves—" Huon started.

A fourth crack opened on the final side.

"Up," I finished for him.

"Up is good," he agreed.

I snapped my wings open, but snatched them back as a burst of steam shot out of the river of magic and scalded a tip.

"Shit, that's hot!"

"Try again!" Huon insisted. He spread his wings and winced as the steam rose to meet them.

"I don't think it wants us to leave!" I said.

"That's a good reason why we should," he said. "Come on!" He tugged on my hand insistently.

The ground shifted under my feet and I almost fell. Only Huon's hand kept me from falling. He stood with his legs apart, steadying us both.

"Wings, Summer!"

I forced my wings back out and flapped in spite of the pain.

Together, we leapt skyward, Kale a handspan behind. We flew several metres up and hovered over the cracks.

They grew longer until they met, forming a circle of molten, golden magic. It would have been pretty if it wasn't as terrifying as shit.

"Is this what really happened to lesser magic?" I asked no one in particular. "It got sucked away and then…" I shook my head.

Neither Fae answered.

The ground shook again. The cracks became wider and wider.

"We should warn the others, we need to get them out of here," I said. Was the key in there somewhere? Had it melted in the shining furnace I created? If it was gone, then our journey was done, failed.

Fucked.

We'd doomed the realms.

I doomed them.

I felt as though my heart might shatter into a thousand pieces.

"It's my fault," I said to myself.

A tree groaned and sank into the magic.

The crack widened. At this rate, it would swallow the island in a matter of hours.

"Yes, we should go—" Huon started.

"Wait," Kale called out.

From the centre of the circle of magic, the ground began to rise.

CHAPTER TWENTY-ONE

"**W**ell, that was unexpected," Huon remarked.

"That's certainly one way to put it, yes," I agreed.

"It makes sense something like this would remain hidden under the island all this time," Kale said.

I looked sidelong at him. "You say that as though you expected to see it."

"I didn't expect it," he said slowly. "But now it's made itself known to us, I understand its presence."

"That's good," I replied. "If you'd known but hadn't said so, I think I would be justified in socking your arm."

He gave me a wan smile. "Indeed, I would deserve it. Rest assured, I thought we were as—as screwed as you believed us to be."

Huon chuckled at Kale's words. "It looks like the rest of us are rubbing off on you, buddy." He patted Kale's arm. "So, I guess it's safe to go inside?"

I eyed the enormous stone structure which had risen out of the ground in the centre of the ring of magic.

It was like nothing I ever saw before. Made from black stone, the sun shone across its surface. Here and there, veins of silver or gold shot through the stone.

A narrow doorway beckoned, about as tempting as boiling magic.

If anything ever said, 'For more danger, enter here,' it was this place. Even though it hadn't moved for the last hour, I wouldn't rule out the earth sucking it back down the moment anyone crossed the threshold.

"Everywhere Summer goes, erections happen," Saff said as he stepped out of the trees nearby.

I gave him a watery smile. "I'm not going to rate that, this was terrifying."

Saff nodded. "The whole island rocked. We figured you three had something to do with it. We're fine, by the way."

I blushed and moved to embrace him and

Fletcher. Tavar already stepped away to examine the newly risen tower.

"I'm sorry, I just freaked out when that shot up out of the dirt. I thought something malevolent sucked in magic to destroy the island, and us." I leaned into Saff as he snaked an arm around me, tucking me close to his side.

"I wouldn't rule out malevolence just yet," Huon said. He gestured toward Fletcher. "Have you ever seen anything like this before?"

Fletcher shook his head. "Only in movies and on TV." He glanced around. "Rick and Jude aren't with you?"

"No." I frowned. To be honest, I'd forgotten about them and Yina. "Khat was here, but he took off when the ground shook. He hasn't slunk back yet. I haven't seen any sign of the others. I'm sure they're fine," I added hastily.

"I'm sure they are," he agreed. He didn't look certain, but he smiled and followed Tavar. Apparently, their curiosity already overcame their caution.

"I gather you didn't find anything interesting on the other side of the island?" I asked Saff.

He shook his head. "Not really. Just the remains of what looked like an ancient quarry. I guess they mined the stone for this tower there."

That suggested a lot of thought and planning went into the creation of this tower and the magic which bound it underground. Were we the ones the ancients pictured when they did all this? Would they have had faith we could release lesser magic? Perhaps they pictured noble warriors or learned scholars. Fae with grand ambitions and abilities. A bevy of princes and their entourage.

Instead they got a young king, a Fae who rarely took anything seriously, a human, a troll, a talking cat and me. Kale, at least, was a scholar. The rest of us were a mishmash, trying to do our best in spite of all the obstacles which popped up—literally and figuratively—in our way.

"Are we going inside, or are you planning to stand around until dust gathers?" Tavar asked.

"I don't have a problem with dust," I muttered. I sucked in a breath and let it out through pursed lips. "But we should go in before a boatload of people turn up." I couldn't answer the questions I had, much less those of any newcomers.

I looked around at the face around me. Faces I adored and respected. I couldn't bear the idea of losing any of them. We'd been through too much already.

"My magic did this, and my blood," I said slowly. "I suppose that means I should go in first."

"When the island rocked, I felt myself drawn to you, like you needed me," Saff said softly. "I still feel like that. If you're going first, I'm going with you."

I smiled and leaned over to kiss his mouth. Gods, I wanted to run away with him, with all my guys, and hide under a bush. The tower had waited this long, it could wait a little longer. Right?

I gripped Saff's arm and the taut muscle beneath his shirt. I deepened the kiss, lost in the moment for a few heartbeats.

Tavar cleared her throat and drew me back to reality with a crash.

I pulled back from Saff and gave her a flat look. She returned it with an unapologetic one.

"You're the one who mentioned a boatload of people," she reminded me.

I nodded. "I guess the legends passed on from troll to troll didn't mention a tower like this?"

"No," she replied, "but the stones look to have been cut and placed in a similar manner to the ruins in the Fae realm."

I squinted at the tower. "You're right." The stone itself was different, but the size of the stones and the even placement was strikingly similar.

"Not entirely surprising since they were built at around the same time," Kale remarked. "We should watch for doors with symbols on them."

"And trapdoors." I glanced toward Fletcher, who paled at the mention of the strange symbol which had transported both of us inside the tunnels where the dark magic objects lay hidden.

"You can stay out here if you like," I said softly.

He blinked at me a few times as though trying to clear the memory out of his head. "Wherever ever you go, I go," he replied.

I wouldn't push the matter. I wanted him to come with me.

I gave a nod. "Great. Stay close to Saff and I. Kale and Huon, you should be in the middle and Tavar, you can watch our backs."

"Very well," she replied.

I caught Huon grinning at me.

"What?" I asked him.

"Sometimes I wonder who is king here," he replied. He didn't seem annoyed at all, just amused.

"Do you have a better idea?" I gestured toward the tower.

He held up his hands. "Not at all. Actually, it's hot when you take charge."

"I second that," Saff said. "She could do it more often. I would follow her."

"I third it," Fletcher said. "But to me, she is always hot."

"I also agree, but as Summer suggested, we should hurry," Kale said. He cocked an eyebrow and looked at each of us in turn.

My face was bright red by now. I took the opportunity to turn away and march toward the tower. I wasn't used to praise, especially not like this. I liked it, but at the same time, it was embarrassing. At least Khat wasn't present to make fun of me. Thank the gods for small mercies.

"Leaving without me?" I heard his voice before I saw him slink back toward us. "Just so you know, I heard all of that and I threw up in my mouth a little. I've hacked up furballs which were less cringey."

Khat paused and then, in Huon's voice, said, "If she told me to tear off all my clothes and run around naked, I'd do it." Then in Saff's, "If only my brain was half as smart as my cock, I would—"

"All right," I snapped, "that's enough. You could have stayed in the Fae realm and waited for us to save your sorry, furry ass. But no, you chose to come because you couldn't help yourself. Unless you can think of something useful to say, then for the love of the gods, shut the hells up."

Khat gaped. He flopped down on his ass, his ears twitched, tail flicked back and forth.

"Fine," he said simply. He rose and walked with chin and tail in the air, to stand behind Tavar.

I didn't think for a minute he was really cowed, but he might give us a break for a while.

"For the record, my brain is at least as smart as my cock," Saff said cheerfully.

"Of course it is," Huon said and clapped him on the back. "And it's almost as much fun."

Khat coughed.

I ignored him, took Saff's arm and stepped toward the tower.

"You're trembling," he said softly.

"Can you blame me?" I asked. "After the vault where we found the first key almost fell on us, then this almost killed us as it shot out of the ground. It seems as though this whole quest is trying to kill us."

"We've made it this far," he replied, more serious than I ever heard him. "We're still alive and more or less sane, depending on who you ask."

I snorted softly. "It doesn't seem as though Khat would agree."

Saff waved a hand in dismissal. "Who cares what he thinks? All he's done is make snarky comments and insult us."

"He knew when Myrta was inside my head," I pointed out. Of course I now felt bad for having rounded on the mimicat. We should all have each other's backs, even his. He *tried* to warn the others. He might be the only one capable of sensing her when she came for us again. I had no doubt she would, and soon. We would need him then.

"That's true," Saff conceded, her expression unusually somber. "He said something was up, but it took me too long to realise he was right. I should have listened to him from the start."

"Yes, you should," Khat agreed. He wound past the others and stepped beside me to peer into the tower. "I suppose you want to know if I sense any danger inside there?"

"That would be helpful, yes," I agreed dryly. "So, do you?"

Khat sniffed. For a moment I thought he would refuse to tell us.

Finally, he said, "I sense something, but not evil. Although, not good either."

"Well that's clear," Saff remarked.

I gave him a look to silence him.

Khat's tail whipped against my leg, but he went on. "Whatever is in here, we should be careful, that's a given. It doesn't mean us any immediate harm, but it won't help us. If we're the right ones, then it's indifferent."

"And if we're the wrong ones?" I asked.

"Then we're screwed, most likely," he replied. "But what's new? And no, I'm not talking about cocks this time."

"Kale is the foretold," I reminded him. "Surely that makes us the right ones?"

"Perhaps. Perhaps not. I wouldn't take anything for granted."

I sighed. "You're right, neither would I. We should be ready for anything. At least, as ready as we can be."

"Did you just say to expect the unexpected?" Huon leaned forward so his chin almost touched my shoulder.

"I suppose I did," I sighed. "What choice do we have?"

He kissed my cheek, then said, "None I can think of. Lead on, my queen."

I turned around and knitted my brows, but he

merely smiled back and gestured for me to step inside.

I shrugged and turned back. We could talk about that later. Assuming there was a later.

"All right, here goes nothing," I muttered.

I took a step inside.

CHAPTER TWENTY-TWO

I stepped far enough inside for the others to file in behind me and before I stopped and waited.

The ground remained still. The tower didn't fall in on us.

Yet.

"Any sign of the key?" I whispered. Inside the tower was dark, apart from a rectangle of light which shone through the doorway. We stayed close to it. Evidently none of us was eager to venture any deeper.

"It's close," Kale replied softly.

"Why are we whispering?" Saff asked, his voice as low as Kale and I.

"It seems like the right thing to do," I replied.

Huon nodded his agreement. "Maybe the gods won't hear us."

"That's illogical," Khat said loudly. "Omniscient beings see and hear everything."

"Then you don't need to shout," I hissed at him. I exhaled through my nose and spoke in a normal volume. "We could use some light in here, but I'm not sure we should use more magic."

"The tower fed off magic," Kale said reasonably. "If it does so again, we might presume it needs it to further expose the key to us."

"I suppose that's possible," I agreed reluctantly.

"One of us can try," Huon said. "You've been through enough as it is."

I wasn't sure if I should bristle or be grateful. I wasn't a fragile flower, but I also didn't want to feel magic rushing through me like that again if I could help it.

"It might only be my magic it wants," I said slowly. "And my blood." I shuddered.

Huon put an arm around me and squeezed my shoulders. "It might, but it might not. There's only one way to find out."

I nodded, but said, "Remember how I'll haunt you if you get us killed."

He smiled. "I look forward to being haunted by you some day, but it won't be today."

"You sound very sure of that," I said.

He cocked his head. "I do, don't I? I've been practicing trying to sound authoritative."

"I've noticed that," I told him.

"Oh, you have?" He looked pleased.

"Yes, you're sounding more kingly these days. Is kingly even a word?" I cocked my head in question.

"If it wasn't, it is now," he said firmly. He released me and stepped toward the darkness. "Be ready to run if this goes badly."

"Yes, your highness." I gave him a bow and stepped back toward the doorway.

I caught his snort of amusement. It was punctuated by light which appeared on his hand and illuminated the space around him. He looked expectant.

If the tower objected to his magic, it gave no immediate sign. No shudder, no sudden collapse. That was encouraging.

"It's larger in here than I suspected," Kale remarked.

Only once he said that, it occurred to me to look around. I took a few steps away from the doorway and scanned the walls around us. They looked the same as the outside walls, simple, unadorned stone.

"It looks emptier than I expected," I said. "There's no pool of souls, no pedestal with a key on top, nothing."

"Are you sure the key is here, Kale?" Huon asked.

"So the first key believes," Kale replied.

"Maybe there's a secret tunnel?" Fletcher suggested. "Or—" He swallowed loudly. "A trapdoor."

I almost jumped, before I realised I wasn't standing on anything which looked like that. I silently chastised myself for not looking down the moment we entered.

"I don't see one," I said nervously.

"No bottomless pit either," Saff said cheerfully.

"Thank the gods for that," I muttered. "What about that symbol we've found a couple of times, the rose surrounded by knots? Or an anchor?"

"I see neither." Huon raised his hand and turned a slow circle.

I turned too, following the light around the room.

"I find the lack of anything to be extremely suspicious," Tavar remarked.

"As do I," Kale agreed. "We are clearly missing something."

I bit my lip. "Maybe it needs my magic after all?"

"It might, but are you sure you want to try?" Huon asked.

I hesitated, then nodded. "It seems safe enough."

"Famous last words," Khat said.

"Unless you have a better idea?" I asked him. "It might be your magic we need."

"It can suck a bag of catnip," he replied.

"How would anyone—never mind." I raised my hand and hoped no one saw my shaking. I'd used magic, often without thinking, for most of my life. To be scared of it now made my skin itch with annoyance.

"It's all right, Summer," Fletcher said softly. "If anyone can do this, it's you. You're the most badass of us all."

"Speak for yourself," Khat said.

"You *have* a bad ass," Saff told the mimicat. "I've smelled your farts."

"You're one to talk," Khat retorted.

I choked back a laugh and let magic flare on my palm. For a long moment nothing happened. I took a deep breath of relief.

Then some of it shot out and hit the wall in front of me. The stone began to crumble.

"Shit, not again!" I cursed.

"You weren't supposed to blow it up," Huon said as he herded the others toward the door.

"I'm not!" I cried. "I'm just using illumination." I took a few hasty steps back.

"Wait," Saff called. "It's… it's moving aside."

I blinked hard. "What are you…"

"He's right," Fletcher said. "The stone isn't falling in piles, it's dissipating."

"That still doesn't sound good." I peered and, without thinking, took several steps forward, then a few more. Either this was magic, or the stone fell in perfect symmetry. What was left looked to be a doorframe. I was no stonemason, but I was pretty sure things didn't crumble apart so neatly.

The guys were correct, my magic revealed a doorway which lay hidden in the wall.

After a few minutes, the opening was totally clear, and wide enough for us to pass through. But to where?

"Um, so I suppose we're going in there then?" I asked.

"I suspect we should," Saff replied.

"I hope this isn't a bad idea." I let my magic shine into this new corridor.

"It probably is," Khat said, "there's something in there which makes my fur stand on end."

"We should wait," Fletcher said. "The air in there would be stale if it's been enclosed for a thousand years."

"You're scared of stale air?" Saff asked Khat.

"Anyone with sense would be," the mimicat replied. "Stale air can kill."

I looked at Fletcher questioningly. To my surprise, he nodded.

"It's not so much the air as what's in the air," he explained. "Germs and things can build up over time. We should give them a chance to disperse."

"All right. It would suck to get this far and die from ancient germs," I said. "How long do we wait?"

"Not too long," he replied. "I'd give it a few hours, but that proverbial boatload of people might arrive in the meantime. A few minutes will have to do."

"I think I'll wait outside," Khat said. "Someone should be the lookout."

"I prefer you stayed here to warn us against things inside this place." I tried to suppress a shiver, but the longer we stayed here, the more I got the creeps from it. I ran my hand over my hair and thought about it for a moment.

"When we first got here, we were angry with each other," I said slowly. "I haven't felt that since or seen anything to indicate why."

"This place is ancient," Khat said. "It was probably bored out of its mind sitting here all that time. Wouldn't you be pissed off and try to screw with the first people who showed up?"

I frowned at him. "If I was made of stone, I doubt I'd feel anything, much less pissed off."

"What about magic?" he asked, as if the question was supposed to make sense in some way.

"Magic isn't any more alive than stone." Huon sounded impatient. "If you're getting at something, then spit it out."

Khat flicked his tail. "Souls," he said finally. "I'm getting at magic having trapped souls in stone for a thousand years."

"We haven't seen any souls," I said, then looked around again, just in case.

"We didn't see any in the vault either, until we got to the pool," Khat pointed out. "Just because you haven't seen them, doesn't mean they aren't here."

I nodded. "That is possible. You think we're supposed to go inside there in our minds, not just walk on in?" I jerked my head toward the new tunnel.

"Why open the tunnel if we were?" Huon reasoned. "We can try that if there's a dead end."

I shuddered. "Please don't use expressions like that though."

"What, dead end? It just means—"

I interrupted him. "I know what it means, but it has the word *dead* in it, so please don't go there."

He held up a hand. "Sorry, I'll keep that in mind." He turned to Fletcher. "Have we waited long enough yet?"

Fletcher glanced at his watch. "I think so, yes." He looked toward me.

"I'm going first," I declared. Before anyone could speak, I hurried toward the tunnel, magic in my palm to light the way.

"Me too." Saff hurried to catch up.

I glanced over my shoulder to see Kale and Huon right behind. Fletcher and Tavar brought up the rear, while Khat wove himself between them all.

The corridor was nothing special, just a long, narrow space made from the same stone as everything else in this tower. The endless, shining black was becoming tedious.

Clearly the ancients lacked the imagination to throw in some white or even brown here and there. I reminded myself they probably weren't building for looks, but with what stone they had. Still, all the same sameness was depressing.

"We're heading downward." The slope was gentle, but undeniable.

"It might go deep under the island," Huon suggested.

"It could go back to Sydney," Saff said.

"Maybe we'll end up in New Zealand," Fletcher remarked. I couldn't tell if he was joking or not.

"Or it could just be a few metres long and then end suddenly," I said.

"Has it?" Fletcher asked.

"Not yet," I replied. "I have a funny feeling this is going to go a long way down. Kale, are we getting closer to the key, or further away?"

"I don't know," he replied. "All I feel is that it's somewhere around here."

"That's remarkably unhelpful," Khat said.

"It's the best I can do," Kale said unapologetically. "Finding magic keys isn't an exact science. Perhaps you can do better?"

I stopped to look at Khat.

He looked back at me.

"I can't, but I'm not the foretold," he replied.

"All right then." I resumed walking. "If you have anything useful to offer, by all means let me know."

"We're travelling downward," Khat said.

"We've established that already." I was starting to

get annoyed with him.

"No, I mean the angle is steeper than it was a few moments ago," he said.

"Oh," I replied. He was right, we were. What did that mean though?

"It's also a straight line," he added.

"So far," I agreed.

"And the floors are paved, but they're getting rougher," he said.

I lowered my hand and looked toward the ground. "It was paved earlier, " I said. Now it was smooth stone, but not in blocks. Up ahead, it looked as though we'd be walking on dirt.

"Maybe they ran out of stone?" Fletcher suggested.

"It's possible," Huon agreed. "We shouldn't read too much into this."

"Right," I agreed, "dragging stone down here would have taken a lot of time and energy."

"And maybe they simply…" Khat stopped.

"What?" Huon asked.

"Shhh," the mimicat insisted. "Listen."

A clicking sound filled the tunnel, soft at first, then growing quickly. It seemed to be coming straight toward us.

I raised my hand. "What the hells?"

CHAPTER TWENTY-THREE

*W*hatever lumbered toward us was enormous. As were the pincers it held out in front of itself.

Click. Click.

It snapped the air. The gigantic body was covered in a kind of shell, which shone a greasy grey in the light of my magic.

"And maybe they got eaten," Khat remarked.

The creature moved closer.

"It looks like a lobster," Fletcher remarked. "But I think it's blind."

"It seems to hear us," Kale said.

"There's not enough room to get past those pincers," Huon replied. "We'll have to shrink it down and step past."

I nodded and moved aside to let Huon do that.

He raised his hand and magic shot out. It bounced off the shell and struck the wall. A couple of stones shrank and fell out of the wall.

"Oops," Saff said.

A crack appeared in the wall above the newly made hole.

Click. Click.

The lobster drew closer. Its head swung back and forth as if it might sniff us out.

Huon gestured for us all to head back up the tunnel.

"I'm going to stay and try again," he said in my ear.

"If you're staying, I'm staying," I told him.

He frowned at me but aimed again. His brow creased in concentration.

"There has to be a weak spot."

The lobster snapped at the air. Its long tail swung out behind it, dangerously close to the gap Huon made. If it hit that, it might bring down the whole tunnel on us. And itself.

"Behind its head?" I suggested.

"It isn't keeping it still for long enough," Huon growled in frustration.

"Be ready," I said, then darted out ahead of him.

"Hey, you!" I shouted out. I waved my hands in front of me, just in case.

"Summer, what the hells?" Huon called out.

I ignored him.

The lobster turned its head toward me.

"Over here, come and get me!" I shouted. "Come on, look this way."

Click. Click.

The lobster advanced.

A stream of magic passed me and struck the lobster right between one section of shell and another.

The lobster shuddered. It let out a pitiful cry, as though it was in pain.

I lowered my hands and my heart went out to it.

Until it grunted and lunged at me.

I squealed and jumped back. The pincers missed me by a hair. I ran backward a few steps, not game to take my eyes off the creature. Huon grabbed me before I backed into him.

"How is that possible?" I asked. "Magic does nothing."

"I have no idea." He pulled me back. "The ancients might have done something to it."

"I guess so." I shrugged. I don't suppose it

mattered who did this. The fact was, it was done. "We still need to get past."

We retreated to where the others waited for us.

I grabbed Fletcher immediately. "We need to shrink and fly past."

He gave me a nod, no questions needed, and put his arms around me. His trust in me warmed my heart. I hoped it wasn't misplaced.

I shrank us, while Tavar traveled with Kale. Saff and Khat got stuck together.

Barely bigger than a grain of rice, I flew us as close to the ceiling as I could without slamming us into it.

The now enormous lobster reached the place we'd stood moments earlier. It stopped to sniff, clearly confused.

"I never thought I'd be flying with a Fae to get away from a huge lobster," Fletcher whispered.

"It's not on my list of things I expected to do either," I replied. "Don't humans eat those things?"

"When we can afford it," he replied. "That one would feed a small army."

"It's probably not alone either," I said.

He stiffened. "Good point."

The lobster turned in a circle. Its tail struck the

wall. Chips of stone dislodged and fell to the ground with a clatter. This only further confused the creature, who whirled toward the sound.

"There is something in the realms dumber than Saff." Khat's head peeked out from the front of Saff's shirt.

"That would be you," Saff said cheerfully. "You're the one insulting the Fae who is keeping you in the air above that thing."

Khat hissed and disappeared.

I snorted softly and followed Huon deeper into the tunnel.

We flew slowly now, as carefully and silently as we could. Where the ground sloped, so did the roof. Several times I almost hit my head, or bumped Fletcher against the side wall.

"The key is near," Kale whispered loudly.

At the same moment, I had the peculiar sensation of being dragged forward.

It was nothing physical, no hand or rope, nothing I could see or hear.

I fought it for a moment, but the tug was unrelenting.

"What in the name of the gods?" Kale breathed. "I can no longer feel it."

"I can," I replied, confused and slightly scared. "It's pulling me toward it."

"Are you sure that's the key?" Fletcher asked.

I looked him in the eyes and shook my head. "I'm not sure at all, but it's there and it wants me. Needs me." I couldn't have resisted the pull if I wanted to.

"It's close."

The tunnel widened. A room opened up in front of us. The ceiling was higher than my magic light could reach, and the floor lower.

"Ah, we've found the bottomless pit at last," Saff replied.

I murmured my agreement. That was what it looked like.

I flew further down and swung my hand back and forth slowly. My eyes followed the magic as I searched for the floor. There must be one, in spite of our joking about abysses.

We dropped, lower and lower, past the level of the floor in the tunnel.

The tug grew more insistent.

"We're close, but..." I shook my head.

"Maybe it's not on the ground?" Fletcher suggested.

I blinked at him. "You're right." I soared closer to the wall and scanned across it with my hand.

Stone, stone, more black stone. This was undressed, raw stone. Some force had blasted it away, possibly longer than a thousand years ago.

"It reminds me of a lava tube," Fletcher commented. "Although there are no volcanoes in this part of Australia."

"Yet," I said absently.

"Um, yes, yet," he agreed. "I wonder if we're under the tower. You said the magic looked like lava. It could have passed up through here, like a lava tube."

"I suppose so," I agreed. Truthfully, I didn't care where we were, I just wanted to get the key and get the bloody hells out of here. Especially because if this was a tube for anything dangerous, it wasn't a place I wanted to be if it flowed again.

"What is that?" he asked after a few moments of silence.

"What is what?" I stopped and hovered.

He pointed toward the wall a few metres away. "That, there."

I squinted. "I don't see—" I took us over closer.

There, sitting in a pocket in the rock was a golden sphere twice the size of my head. Across the surface, symbols were etched, lines, swirls, a flower here, a triangle there.

"I'm going to suggest it's not a coincidence this is sitting there," I said.

"I think you're right," Fletcher agreed. "Can you feel the key nearby?"

"I... I think it's inside that," I said uncertainly. "I'm going to have to make us bigger, so I can pick it up. I don't think it's supposed to be that big."

"Balls *are* usually pretty big if they can fit in a hand," Fletcher agreed.

I snorted softly. "I'm giving that a nine because I needed a joke to ease the tension."

"Yes!" he said triumphantly. His voice echoed up and down the tube.

"Stop sounding as if you're having fun," Saff said from where he hovered a few metres away.

"I'm always having fun," Fletcher replied. "Who doesn't want to hang out in a tube full of giant crustaceans?"

"Um, me," I replied. I shook my head and grew us until the ball fit in my palm.

"Kale, Tavar?" I called over my shoulder. "Do I just pick this up?" I glanced upward. If this was like the vault where we'd found the first key, the ceiling might collapse the moment I touched it.

Kale flew in closer. "If the key wants you, then you should take it."

I swallowed. "All right then. Here goes." My hand shook. I reached out and curled my fingers around the sphere.

Nothing discernible happened, except an increase in the pull which guided me here in the first place. That became a demand.

Pick me up, take me from this place.

There were no words, but the meaning was clear.

I picked up the sphere and almost dropped it as a scream echoed through the tube. I fumbled it into a pocket and clung to Fletcher.

The scream sounded again.

"Screamspinner?" Fletcher asked.

"Souls!" Huon shouted.

I looked toward his voice. Sure enough, dozens of them surged down from somewhere above us, arms outstretched, mouths open in misty masks of rage.

They screamed again, a multitude of furious voices which echoed and bounced back several times before they faded. The sound seemed to pass through my ears and into my blood, turning it to ice.

I shivered. Had I not held Fletcher so tightly, I would have clapped my hands over my ears.

"You dare to steal from us?" One of the souls came to a halt at the same level as my face.

"We need the key," I replied, my tone as even as I could make it. "It wants me to have it."

The spokes-soul raised a semi-transparent hand and pointed a finger at me. "You lie," it hissed. "The key and the orb have lain here, under our protection for a millennia. We are charged to keep it here. We will not fail our charge."

I licked my lips. "You had to stay and await the foretold. You haven't failed at all. You've done great." I tried to smile, but only bared my teeth. Even that faded when the soul replied.

"Against our wills!" they wailed. "We have waited a millennia. Kept in torment. Those who disturb our purgatory must suffer as we have suffered."

"Um." Oh gods, had these souls gone crazy after all this time? Was that even possible? "We came to release you from your torment."

The soul paused. "Only the foretold can release us. Are you the foretold?"

"The key called to me," I reasoned. "So—yes." Hopefully that would be enough to let them go off into the afterlife and we could get the hells back into the sunshine.

"Prove it," the soul hissed. "We need proof you are the foretold. If you cannot give this to us, then you will take our place and guard the eighth hell."

The eighth hell? After a thousand years here, I'd probably see it like that too.

"How do I prove it to you?" I asked. "The key brought me here. I don't know what else you need." I thought as quickly as I could, but came up blank. Panic started to rise. If I didn't think of something quickly, I would damn us all. The worlds would end, and no one would come to release us.

Ever.

"Give me your hand," the soul insisted. They held out theirs, smoky and thin. The soul hadn't had a physical body for so long. Did they even remember how it felt? Had they had a family? Friends? Were some of them trapped in here as well?

I cast a glance to the side. The souls had arrayed themselves around us, like the humans in Darling Harbour, but without their phones.

I swallowed hard.

"Fletcher, hold on hard to me." Over my shoulder, I added, "Huon, be ready to grab him if you have to."

"I'm ready." Huon was closer than I'd thought. That was heartening.

My hand shook, but I held it out toward the soul.

The soul hovered for a few moments. Long enough that I thought it changed its mind. If it had a mind to change.

Then it surged toward me and grabbed my fingers in its icy grip.

CHAPTER TWENTY-FOUR

*E*verywhere I looked was green, lush. The trees were big and healthy. Each one was decorated with fruit or flowers. The fragrances filled the air, a divine perfume from nature.

I inhaled the scents and picked up my skirt so I could run across the grass. The soft blades tickled the soles of my bare feet.

"Papa, Mama, you're home." I stopped short.

With them was a woman with long blonde hair and a stern face.

"Lady Myrta." I gave her a curtesy, as low as I could.

When I rose again, her expression hadn't changed. She looked displeased. I had never seen her look otherwise, so I dismissed it. This day was too beautiful to let a grumpy old woman ruin it.

"Rosette." Mama's eyes looked troubled. "Run along and play, there's a good girl."

"But I wanted to see if Papa bought me a present. He always—"

"Rosette," Papa snapped. "Your mother said to go and play."

Papa rarely used that tone of voice with me. When he did, I hurried to comply. I hated nothing more in the world than when he became cross with me.

"At once, Papa." I gave Myrta another curtesy and darted off.

Once I was hidden by a tree or two, I stopped and ducked down. I thought they might go inside, but they started on a slow walk around the garden instead.

All the better for me to listen.

"The experiments are going well," Myrta was saying.

Experiment? I frowned to myself, but stayed to hear more.

"Excellent," Mama said. "How long should it be until we..." They walked behind a bush and I couldn't hear what she was saying.

I kept low and followed after them.

"…within the year we should have the first ones," Myrta said. "Cyrir and I are are pleased with the…"

Cyrir must be Lord Cyrir. I met him once or twice. He seemed nice enough, especially compared to Myrta. He didn't seem to like her much. I could never figure out why those who didn't care for each other stayed together. Maybe these experiments had something to do with it.

"Very good," Papa's voice was suddenly close. "We look forward to having the help to maintain the house. Having to pay was always such a—" He stopped suddenly.

"Rosette?" He had that tone again. "Show yourself."

I swallowed and considered staying hidden behind the bush. After a moment, I popped my head up and smiled.

"Oh, I didn't see you there," I said brightly. "I was, um, picking flowers."

My hands were empty.

Papa looked down his nose at me. "Rosette, it's naughty to eavesdrop and worse to lie."

"The child is obnoxious," Myrta snapped. "She should be beaten more often. Or—" She paused. "Perhaps she can help with the experiments."

Mama gasped. "Lady Myrta, no! You cannot mean to take her—"

"I do mean to," Myrta replied. "She can help to create the new breed of Fae."

"My daughter was not born to breed slaves," Papa said. He sounded scared. I had never heard that tone in his voice before. It terrified me.

"Papa, I don't want to go." I grabbed his arm and dug my fingers in. "Please don't let her take me."

Papa looked beseechingly at Myrta. "Please, lady, she meant no disrespect. She really wouldn't be—"

"The decision is made," Myrta said. "I will be leaving now and the brat will come with me. Willingly, or bound, it makes no difference to me."

Mama let out a sob. "Please..."

Myrta ignored her.

Papa pried my fingers from his arm.

"We will do our duty to Fae kind," he said formally. "For the good of Fae kind." When he looked at me again, it was with cold eyes, as though he had already forgotten who I was.

My heart broke into at least a thousand pieces and scattered on the winds and in the grass. Wherever I went, it would always be here. Home, even if I never returned.

"I will go," I whispered. "If Mama and Papa wish it."

Papa nodded, but Mama turned her face. I never saw her eyes again as long as I lived. The next time I saw her, they were closed in death and I had become the monster Myrta made me.

Breeder of slaves, mother of trullen.

Nympha.

~

I jerked back to the present and stared at the soul.

"You're Rosette," I stated softly. "That was your memory."

"Yes," the soul replied. "That was the beginning. That was the moment my soul was dammed to this torment for a thousand years."

"You were a child," I said in horror. "How old were you? Fourteen? Fifteen?"

"I was thirteen," Rosette replied. "I went willingly and did unspeakable things."

"Because she made you do it," I said.

"Because I wanted to," Rosette insisted. "I thought it would make Papa proud. Maybe then he would let me return home."

She sounded so sad I wanted to weep for her. "That was all you really wanted? To go home? Did you?"

She shook her head. "Not really. Myrta became my mentor. I lived with and *for* her. But I knew what we did was wrong. We created tortured beasts."

Tavar cleared her throat. She and Kale hovered nearby, listening.

"I am no beast," Tavar said coldly.

Rosette regarded her. "You may not be, but your ancestors were. Hideous, angry, reviled, enslaved, miserable. We angered the gods themselves by creating the trullen and in turn they placed us here, to safeguard the key and to suffer the slow passing of the years."

"And now you're free," I said, hopefully. "Just let us take the key and you can go. You can rest at last."

Rosette looked at me, her expression intense. "When you saw my memories, I saw yours. You are indeed the foretold for *this* key. However, your journey is still long and will be arduous and fraught. You will need help. When you do, you have the orb."

"Oh? How do we—oh..." Rosette was gone, and with her the oppressive mood I hadn't realised hung over me until now. I put my arm back around Fletcher and shook my head to clear it.

"Are you all right?" he asked. "The souls are all gone."

"Hmmm? Yes, we just need to get out of here," I replied.

Predictably, the tube rumbled and shook.

"Why can't they just let things stand?" I muttered. I was tired, but I flew us up in the direction we came.

"When people find this island, the tower will pose more questions than answers," Fletcher replied.

"If people find the island," I replied, "the whole thing might well sink into the sea."

He swallowed audibly. "We need to find Rick before that happens."

"He's probably in the boat already," I said. "With Jude and Tiny."

"Yeah, I guess so." He didn't look convinced. "We'll find out soon enough."

"Right, I'll need to shrink us again, to get past the—"

A crack opened up above us and daylight poured in.

"Or we could just go out that," I finished. I ducked as a chunk of stone dropped past my head.

"Shit, we don't need that on top of everything," I muttered.

The crack widened and pieces of stone rained

down on us.

"Summer?" Huon sounded worried. He'd made himself bigger and hovered a metre from Fletcher and me.

"I'm fine!" I called back.

I let out a squeak as a particularly large chunk of stone fell and struck Huon on the shoulder. He cried out and dropped out of sight.

"Huon!" I screamed and almost let go of Fletcher in the process.

Stone rained down faster now. It showered my face with dust and filled my nose and eyes.

"We have to get out of here!" Kale shouted.

"Not without Huon!" I yelled back.

"Summer, we need the key," Fletcher said softly.

I looked at him, horrified. "We can't just leave him."

"He'd want you to get to safety." Fletcher turned his face upward. "We're almost there."

He was right, we were only a few metres from the crack.

I made up my mind and gave him a curt nod. I flew us both out of the top of the black tower. The sides crumbled away, piece by piece. It would stand for a matter of minutes, if I guessed correctly.

I followed Kale and Saff a safe distance from the

tower and let Fletcher down. Before anyone could say a word, I pulled the golden orb from my pocket and pressed it into Kale's hand.

"Keep it safe," I said and leapt back into the sky.

"Summer—" Kale began.

"I'm not leaving without Huon," I said firmly. "Stay here, keep the keys safe." Without waiting for a response, I headed back toward the tower and dropped through the ever widening crack.

"Huon?" I called out into the darkness.

I descended slowly, eyes scanning down and around.

"Huon?" I called again, louder this time.

"Summer?" Saff's voice came from above me.

"Saff, you should have stayed out there," I growled at him.

His white teeth flashed in the gloom. "You didn't think I'd let you come alone, or leave Huon here, did you?"

"I suppose not." I sighed. "You're as thick headed as me."

"That sounds about right," he agreed. "Come on, let's find this king of ours." He paused for a moment, then added, "Gods, I hope this wasn't really a bottomless pit."

"I'm sure it has a bottom somewhere," I replied.

Saff snorted. "All this talk of bottoms should be arousing, but frankly this place is terrifying. There's the tunnel we came in through."

I murmured my acknowledgement. We passed the place where I'd found the orb and continued down, magic on our hands to light the way.

The tube shook hard. Stone rained harder than ever. The crack widened further still.

"I think the tower is going to spilt in two," Saff said.

"I think you're right," I replied. "But this section will probably fall in on itself. Huon! Are you there?"

"Summer?" His voice, faint and weak, came back to me.

"Huon?" Saff called. "Hang on, we're coming." After half a minute, he said, "Oh look, there really is a bottom."

Huon lay at the side of the tube. Water covered him to his neck.

"You shouldn't have come back in," he croaked and coughed.

I landed a metre from him, up to my waist in frigid water. The ground underneath was slippery and uneven. I struggled to get my balance and keep it. Between my wings and my arms, I managed the few steps to Huon's side.

"You're welcome," I said sarcastically. "Let's all get the hells out of here."

A section of tower crumbled and landed in the water with a splash. It missed hitting Huon and me by a hair.

"I'm so tired of falling rock," I said under my breath. I hooked an arm under Huon's shoulder and waited for Saff to do the same. "On three. One. Two. Three." We heaved Huon out of the water.

He let out a groan. One arm and one wing hung limply at his side.

"I can't fly," he said, his voice laced with pain.

"Luckily we can," I replied. Neither Saff nor I could risk hanging on to him as he was though. He was clearly not strong enough to cling to either of us.

"I'm going to shrink you," I told him. "You're going to have to travel down the front of my shirt."

"At last," he laughed weakly.

"I broke a fingernail," Saff remarked.

"You can fly yourself," I told him.

He pouted, but leapt up out of the water as I tucked Huon in between my breasts. I held on with one hand and soared up through the tube toward the beckoning sunlight.

CHAPTER TWENTY-FIVE

"*T*hat was reckless and foolish," Huon railed. "In all the time I've known you, that was hands down the stupidest thing you've ever done. Both of you." He looked from me to Saff, eyes narrowed in anger.

"At some point, he'll get to the part where he thanks us for saving his ass," Saff said out of the corner of his mouth.

"You risked your own," Huon growled. "Both of you are important to this journey. Have we not already established that fact? I am not." He sucked in a breath as Khat licked his wing.

"I told you healing magic is slow and painful," Khat said unapologetically.

"Yes, yes," Huon waved his good hand. "Please just get on with it."

"You *are* important," I told him. "You're important to us. To me. I wasn't going to leave you to die."

"You should have," Huon said insistently. He let out a long breath. "But thank you for saving my ass."

"And the rest of you," Saff said.

"And the rest of me," Huon agreed.

Satisfied he was more or less all right, I turned back toward the tower. It continued to crumble, but the destruction had slowed somewhat. Of course it had, it probably waited for us to get clear first, just to be a dick.

Still, it hadn't stopped falling and I doubted it would until nothing but rubble remained.

"All right then, we need to find the others and a way back to the Fae realm. One more key and we're done." I smiled, but this journey was far from over.

"You'll need this." Kale handed me the orb. "The first key is excited. I think it wants to see the second."

I took the orb and looked closely at it. In the sun, it was easier to make out the symbols etched in the sides. I was sure they all meant something, but I was too tired right now to even consider what.

"It has hinges," I remarked. "I guess that means it

opens here." On the opposite side, in the centre of the joints that made up the two halves of the orb, was a small groove.

I slid my fingernail into the groove and wiggled it back and forth. The orb gave a click and popped open. There inside, on a bed of green velvet, lay the second key. It winked in the sun as though to say it was happy to meet me.

"So, you're a foretold after all," Kale said softly. I looked up into his eyes. He seemed pleased we both were, rather than annoyed I had taken his special title.

"It seems so," I agreed. "I presume the third key has chosen someone else. Or it will." I nodded toward the other guys.

"That sounds likely," Kale agreed. "It seems we may all be of equal importance." He looked pointedly at Huon.

Huon didn't miss his scrutiny. "It remains to be seen," he replied indifferently. "In the meantime, they were still reckless."

I smirked at him and turned the orb so the key dropped onto my hand. If I didn't know better, I might assume it was an ordinary key. However, I felt its attachment to me. It wanted me or needed me as much as we needed all of the keys.

I slid it into my pocket and scrutinised the orb. I closed it, clicked it shut and rolled it across my palm.

"Rosette said the orb would help in some way," I said slowly. "But it just looks like a pretty bauble."

"It would probably sell for a shit load of money on eBay," Fletcher remarked. "Or maybe it should be in a museum."

I shrugged. "Tavar, have you heard of anything like this before?" I glanced up to see her shake her head.

"Never, but I don't think it's an object of dark magic."

I hadn't thought of that before. Now I did, I almost dropped the orb. I managed to curl my fingers around it at the last moment. For all I knew, if it fell it might break and be of no use to us at all.

"Whatever it is," I said, "we'll work it out later. Maybe the library back home will have the answer."

Home.

Gods, I missed the Fae realm like an ache I hadn't let myself feel until now. The calling to go back was almost as strong as the key tugging me to it.

"Then there's the small matter of getting home," Saff said. "I haven't seen an anchor anywhere." He rubbed the side of his head. "Although I suppose the boat would have one. Maybe not a magical one though."

"I can't go home," Khat said, "I haven't found my mate yet."

"Don't worry," I told him, "we'll go back to the mainland. While we figure out how to get back home, you can search. All right?"

That seemed to appease him. He went back to healing Huon. Rather him than me. Khat's tongue looked rough and the pain intense.

I turned from him to Fletcher. "Let's find Rick first. He can't have gone too far. This island isn't that big."

Just as I said that, the tower gave an enormous rumble and collapsed in on itself. The ground beneath us shook and rolled with the impact. A cloud of dust rose into the afternoon sky.

"We should go before someone comes looking for the source of the earthquake," Fletcher said.

The ground shook again.

"And before we become victims of it," Saff said.

I nodded my agreement. "Huon, can you fly?"

He rolled his shoulders and wings. "I'm a little stiff, but I think I can manage."

"So, about the usual," I teased.

He grinned at me. "Something like that."

He scooped up Khat as I put my arms around Fletcher.

"I could get used to this," Fletcher remarked.

"Flying?" I asked.

"Having your arms around me," he said.

I smiled. "It is nice." I pressed a kiss to his lips.

As if on cue, the island shook again. "Come on, let's find Rick and Jude. And Yina. And Tiny." We couldn't forget the dog, after all.

We leapt skyward into a cloud of dust.

"I'm going to need a good bath after this." I wiped my eyes as they watered.

"I think I'll join you," Fletcher said.

"Me too," Saff called out.

"Me three," Huon added.

All eyes turned to Kale, who merely arched an eyebrow at us and didn't answer.

I shook my head and focused my attention on the ground below us.

"Any sign of them?" I asked Fletcher.

"Not yet," he replied. "They can't be far. There's the boat. There's no one in it."

I followed his arm when he pointed. Someone must have tied the boat, a rope extended from it to somewhere on the island. For now, at least. With every shake, the boat rocked violently. Any more pressure and the rope might snap.

I was less concerned with the watercraft than I was in finding Rick and Jude. We could manage without the boat, even if Rick lost his job in the process. Better that than his life.

Slowly, we circled the island.

"I think those are footsteps." I squinted at marks in the sand. They led toward a series of scrappy bushes, then ended.

Of the two men and the dog, I saw no further sign.

"They can't have just disappeared." I frowned.

"Maybe that's what the orb is for?" Fletcher suggested. "To help with things like this?"

"It's possible," I said uncertainly. I landed us on the beach near the footprints and drew it out of my pocket. I held out my palm and set the orb in the centre.

"I'm not sure what to do now," I admitted.

"Can you ask it to find them?" Saff suggested as he landed nearby.

"Um. Orb, can you find our friends? They're a bit lost. We need to find them and take them home."

As I said the last word, the thought of the Fae realm flickered through my mind.

The world around me began to spin. I felt someone grab my arm. A moment later, someone grabbed the other.

The beach and water became a blur.

With a start, I recognised what was happening. The orb had created a portal.

"No, no, no," I said. My breath was pulled away with each word. "We need to find our friends. We can't go back to the Fae realm yet."

I didn't know who spoke, but the voice was male. "You have the second key. You must seek the third. Your time in the human realm is done, as was foretold."

"But—"

"As was foretold," the voice repeated.

My vision swam and the portal sucked us in. The key in my pocket seemed to sing as we were flung across the veil and back home.

~

I fell to the ground amongst a pile of arms and legs. I grunted with pain as I hit the dirt and someone's knee.

In spite of the discomfort, I lay like that for a good while, eyes closed. My pounding heart slowed.

My head stopped spinning. My breath came back to me.

"Is everyone all right?" That was Huon's voice.

I forced my eyes open a crack. I wished I hadn't. My head ached and the leaves on the trees nearby were brown and rotten. The smell of putrid foliage hit my nostrils. I flared them and swallowed back my stomach contents.

"I'm alive," I said. I managed to sit up.

"I'm here," Saff said. "Summer is on my leg."

"Sorry." I shifted off it.

"I am also here," Kale said. "The first key is safe, in my pocket."

"I still have the second key," I replied. The orb was still cupped in my hand.

"I'm pissed off," Khat declared. "We're back here again. My mate is still stuck in the human realm."

"We are alive," Tavar said firmly. "And closer to the return of lesser magic."

"Yeah, yeah, whatever." Khat stalked off toward the trees. "Shit," he growled when he reached them.

"What?" I rubbed my temples and cocked my head at him.

"We're closer to the Fae capital than I have ever been," he replied.

"No one there is going to eat you—" Huon started.

"No, you dumbass, look at the trees, the taint. It wasn't this close when we left."

"Time moves differently here," I pointed out.

"I know that, but it looks as though we've been gone a lot longer than we intended to," Khat said. "Maybe too late to stop the taint from killing the realm."

"We can't be too late," I replied uneasily. "Surely even if it's spread, we can stop it and reverse it. We just need the last key. Right?"

No one had an answer for me.

"Well fuck," I said.

~

*W*ill they find the third key? Will Summer and Kale ever get to third base? Find out in the third book, Flicker.

ABOUT THE AUTHOR

Maggie Alabaster is a reverse harem and fantasy romance author.

She lives in NSW, Australia with one spouse, two daughters, dog, cat, rabbits and countless birds.

Sign up for my newsletter! Sign Up!

Join my reader group! Join here!

Follow me on Bookbub! Click here to follow me!

ALSO BY MAGGIE ALABASTER

Court of Blood and Binding

Book 1 Song of Scent and Magic

Book 2 Crown of Mist and Heat

Book 3 Sword of Balm and Shadow

Book 4 Whisper of Frost and Flame

Dark Masque

Book 1 Bait

Book 2 Prey

Book 3 Trap

Saving Abbie

Book 1 Pitch

Book 2 Pound

Book 3 Session

Book 4 Muse

Book 5 Rhythm

Book 6 Encore

Novella Venomous

Ruthless Claws

Book 1 Ivory

Book 2 Crimson

Book 3 Elodie

Harmony's Magic

Book 1 Summoned by Fire

Book 2 Summoned by Fate

Book 3 Summoned by Desire

Shifter's Vault

Book 1 Discarded

Book 2 Deceived

Book 3 Disgraced

My Alien Mates

Book 1 Star Warriors

Book 2 Star Defenders

Book 3 Star Protectors

Academy of Modern Magic

Book 1 Digital Magic

Book 2 Virtual Magic

Book 3 Logical Magic

Complete Collection

Summer's Harem

Book 1: Shimmer

Book 2: Glimmer

Book 3: Flicker

Complete collection

Short reads

Taken by the Snowmen

Jingle All the Way

Also by Maggie Alabaster and Erin Yoshikawa

Caught by the Tide

Book 1–Pursued by Shadows

Book 2 Pursued by Darkness

Book 3 Pursued by Monsters